unnerving

twelve unsettling stories plus one

NIGHTFALL

BLUE FORGE PRESS
Port Orchard, Washington

Unnerving Nightfall
Twelve Stories for a Monthly Dose of Shivers
Copyright 2023
by Blue Forge Press

Cover art by Brianne DiMarco

First Print Edition, October 2023
Second Print Edition, October 2023

ISBN 978-1-59092-913-1

For information about film, reprint or other subsidiary rights, contact blueforgegroup@gmail.com

Blue Forge Press is the print division of the volunteer-run, federal 501(c)3 nonprofit company, Blue Legacy, founded in 1989 and dedicated to bringing light to the shadows and voice to the silence. We strive to empower storytellers across all walks of life with our four divisions: Blue Forge Press, Blue Forge Films, Blue Forge Gaming, and Blue Forge Records. Find out more at www.MyBlueLegacy.org

Blue Forge Press
7419 Ebbert Drive Southeast
Port Orchard, Washington 98367
blueforgepress@gmail.com
360-550-2071 ph.txt

this volume is dedicated to
the mushrooms that grow from decay
the phoenix who rise from the ashes
and the beauty we find in the shadows

CONTENT WARNING

This book is intended for mature audiences as these stories are purposefully meant to unsettle the reader. If one month's story is too intense, skip that month. While the editor and Blue Forge Press have selected and edited each of these stories, ultimately you are responsible for curating what you read.

For a full list of triggers by story, please write to:
blueforgepress@gmail.com

table of contents

UNNERVING

twelve unsettling stories plus one

NIGHTFALL

January

Death on the River

Daniel DiQuinzio

he wood comprising my lower left leg felt stiff and heavy as I walked through the cold Wyoming morning; I'd lost my real leg years ago in my Army days. Today is Sunday the 21st of January. Today despite the cold and the snow covering the streets, I am leading my wife and my children towards the local Catholic Church for a funeral. This morning my family is attending the funeral of my old friend Joseph Parker. He died two weeks ago today on the 7th day of January from a heart attack.

Joseph's doctor, Doctor Sullivan, claims my old friend overworked himself on his farm but I know that is not true. Doctor Sullivan did not see what Joseph and I saw on that strange and unnatural ship that we explored the day before Joseph's death. It was shock. Shock caused his heart attack. Shock caused his death. Joseph was so terrified by what we saw onboard that ship that his heart gave out on him.

Since Joseph's death, I have debated with myself if I should tell anyone of our discoveries. Joseph's wife, Sharon, should know the true cause of his death, as should his children. However, I do not know if Joseph's family would believe me. In fact, I do not know if anyone would believe my tale. I must decide whether to speak or stay silent; the walk to the church is not long.

Joseph and I grew up together in a small city in Wyoming. Its name is Casper. Both our fathers came out West from the Eastern states decades ago. They came to seek their fortune.

Joseph's father was a surveyor who worked for the railway. He came out West before the big war that divided the county. In Wyoming, he made his home in Casper. When the war started, he went off to join the Union army.

My father didn't come West until the late 1870s, after his own service in the Union army. He found work in Wyoming. At first, he worked for the railroad as a ticket agent. In that capacity, he met my mother. After several years, he retired to open his own business. Together my parents ran the local grocery store.

Joseph and I met at the Casper schoolhouse. As young men, we idolized our fathers' service in the Union army. We idolized their bravery. Most of all we idolized the causes they fought for which was republicanism, the American way of life and individual rights and liberties.

Joseph and I enlisted in the Army after high school. Its mission was different then it had been for our fathers. The settlers were pouring into the frontiers. As they did, they came into increasing contact with the Native tribes. Now out in the West, war was breaking out between the settlers and the Natives.

After boot camp, we joined the cavalry. The two of us served in several of the wars between the tribes in the West and the U.S. Army. Both of us rose to the grades of cavalry sergeants.

In our last campaign, our regiment rode out in response to the Apache's raiding several of the small towns. Our regiment intercepted their party after a raid. There was a skirmish and during it, I was shot off my horse. My right leg hit the ground hard when I landed. I thought the pain would kill me but I did not die from it. I looked up and saw a pair of braves standing over my body. I shot one with my pistol killing him on the spot. The other he hit me with the bunt of his own rifle. Then he grabbed my head and pulled out his knife.

My leg rose planning to kick him in desperation for I knew what he was going to do to me; he planned to scalp me. Then I a cavalryman rode up on his horse. Before the brave could act, the soldier killed him with a shot from his revolver. It was Joseph. My friend saved my life. Then Joseph put me on his horse and brought me to the medical tent. As he stood watch, the medical officer on duty examined me and determined my right calf was too badly hurt to save. Then and there, the doctor removed my leg with his sawbones. It was that day I gained my wooden leg.

A few months later, I mustered out of the Army. So, too, did Joseph. Afterwards we both went back to Casper. There we met and married our wives. I was employed at my family's grocery store and Joseph worked there along side me. He continued to work at the grocery store after I took it over from my parents.

In time, thought, Joseph tired of the city. He desired to raise a family away from the bustle. He bought a farm in Bessemer Bend. It was located where the farming community over looked the Platte River. At the time, his wife was pregnant with their first child.

Joseph's first child—also his first son—was born shortly after he brought the farm in Bessemer Bend. As soon as his wife and his son were fit to travel, they moved. Joseph and I entered into a little business partnership. His farm provided my wife and me with fresh produce for the store. In turn, I provided him and his wife with a very nice discount whenever their family shopped at there.

After he moved out to Bessemer Bend, we exchanged correspondence and regularly visited each other's homes. This is how I know of the real cause of Joseph's death. The day before Joseph died—the same day that the strange and terrible ship appeared on the Platte River—I was visiting him at his farm.

By coach it was several hours travel time from Casper to Joseph's farm. That day the trip took even longer because of the cold and the snow covering the ground. It was evening when I arrived and Joseph and his wife Sharon greeted me at their front door. They directed me to their guest room and that night I dined with them.

The next morning I woke sometime just after the sun rose. After breakfast, Sharon informed me that Joseph was out working in their back yard. On the way out, I passed his field hands. All of them were veterans.

After a while, I found Joseph. With his axe, he was cutting down a tree. After he saw me approach, he bought down his axe, stowing in a stump next to where he stood.

Joseph invited me inside for drinks with him and Sharon and started to lead me back to their farmhouse. But as we looked out over the frozen water of the Platte River we saw something down near the riverbank.

It seemed to appear suddenly. No one saw it but us. A ship. It was a ship! From Joseph's farm there seemed to be something unnatural and at the same time grim about it and Joseph was intrigued by it. He convinced me that we should investigate. He ordered a pair of horses to be saddled and provisioned. From his gun cabinet we drew and loaded a pair of revolvers and a pair of rifles. Joseph informed Sharon we would be riding down to the bank of the river and we would return later that day.

Then we departed. We rode down to the river. It took us several hours to reach its bank, the cold wind hitting our horses and us.

As we came to the riverbank, we could see the ship better. It possessed three tall masts. Standing atop the masts where three large white sails. The hull of the ship was dark black. That was an unusual color for a hull. At first, Joseph and I thought the ship had run aground. Once we were on the riverbank we stopped our horses. This time of year the Platte River was frozen and the weight of the horses would crack the ice.

We dismounted and tied the reins to a tree. Then with our weapons at the ready, we moved towards the ship for a closer investigation. As we approached the ship, we did not see any sign of a shore party. As we examined the vessel, we could tell its sails were unfurled. Then we heard several noises. Above us, the sails were full and flapping as they were struck by the cold January wind. Yet the ship was not moved.

To me, that made the ship seem all the more alarming. As for Joseph, he was even more intrigued! I tried to convince Joseph we should forget about the ship and return to his farm. My instincts told me this ship was both devilish and evil. Indeed, they also told me that this ship foretold death.

Joseph heard my arguments. He did not agree with me. Instead, he proposed we walk around and if no means could be found to board the ship then we would forget about it and return to his farmhouse. It seemed a reasonable compromise but now I greatly regret it. If I had reasoned with him longer or was firmer in my arguments we would not have seen the ship's ghastly crew and the wicked cargo it carried. But no, instead, we set out.

Joseph led the way and I followed. At first, we moved

down along the ship's starboard hull. We pondered its existence. Joseph was in awe for he was much impressed with its design. With me, the reason was different. Instead, I dreaded this strange unmoving ship and the evil it represented.

As we walked, Joseph and I were able to investigate further. If the ship crashed, there would be wreckage from it that washed ashore. There was none. If the ship ran aground, there would be damage to the ship's ventral hull. There was none. There was also no evidence of any damage to its keel. What was more, we did not see any ice on the keel.

Soon we came to the point where the bank of Platte River gave way to the frozen water of the river. Joseph stopped. I stopped behind him. This was as far as we could go. We dared not walk over the ice in case it gave way under our combined weight.

We stood there. Our eyes looked ahead towards the stern of the ship. From where we stood, we could see there was no sign of an anchor in the water. This ship did not appear to have run aground on the riverbank. There we turned around, walking back they way we came.

In time, we came to the ship's bow. Now I knew this ship could not exist. Its presence violated all known laws of motion and physics. Indeed, it seemed to very ominously *rest* on the riverbank.

In front of the bow of the ship, we debated our next course of action. Joseph wanted to inspect the port hull to see if any entrance could be found along that side. Again, I tried to convince my old friend we should return to his farm and forget about the ship. Once more, he dismissed my concerns. For a second time, we made the same agreement that if we did not find a ladder or some other entrance we would return to his farm.

We moved down the port hull. This time I was in the lead

with Joseph following behind. We were starring up at its hull, standing close to its amidships. Hanging above us was a rolled rope ladder. Joseph pointed his rifle up and caught the tip of its barrel on the bundled ladder. Joseph snagged the rope and the ladder fell down over the port side of the hull. It was decided we would climb onboard and further investigate with Joseph climbing first; I brought up the rear.

It took us a few minutes to climb onto the main deck of the ship. With our rifles out, we examined the deck. At first, we saw no sign of the crew. We moved around until we came to the main mast. Still there was no sign of the crew.

Then from behind the main mast many figures appeared. They walked towards us. At the sight of them, my skin crawled. Joseph's body tensed. I thought I saw sweat as it trickled down his brow.

On instinct, we aimed our rifles at the... *creatures*. Strangely, they did not react to either of us. Instead, they merely continued to move along the main deck. As they moved, we examined them. They were not human, yet they possessed bodies. They possessed the same anatomical outlines and limbs as mortal men and women, in fact. But for some reason, they also lacked any organs or skin. All of them were composed of nothing but bones. They were skeletons. All of them were skeletons. Skeletons the crew of this strange ship. It was another impossible sight. It was physically impossible for the dead to walk—let alone for bones to crew a sailing ship.

Joseph and I moved around them. Still, they did not notice us. As such, we continued exploring the ship. In a few minutes, Joseph and I walked beyond the main mast. As we approached the mizzenmast—the rear mast—we found a large object. For some reason, lying on the deck of a ship that should not exist with a crew that should not exist, there lay a large black coffin. This also should not exist.

Joseph looked into my eyes. In turn, I looked back at him for both of us were pondering the presence of this coffin on this haunting ship. Joseph moved forward. My mouth opened with the intention to stop him but no words came out. It was imperative I stop him. This coffin was very clearly the work of evil. My arms would not move to hold him back.

Joseph was now leaning over the coffin with his rifle. His arms reached down touching the lid. It glowed, seeming to respond to his touch. Then the lid of the coffin slid off. Joseph could see what was within and he did not speak. From where I stood behind him, I watched and heard his rifle drop onto the deck. He just stood there, his body frozen. I approached him and he did not acknowledge my presence. When I spoke to him, he did not reply to me. I looked at him; Joseph's face was very pale and he was sweating heavily. I looked pass him and into the open coffin. Now, I could see what was inside of it. It was a body; it was Joseph's body.

My arms could now move. I retrieved Joseph's rifle. As I handed it to him, he was breathing very rapidly. Sweat drenched his brow.

From Joseph's wide eyes, it was clear now we both desired to leave. We raced back along the main deck of the ship. *The rope ladder,* I thought as we ran. *Please let the rope ladder still be there.* It was our only hope of escaping. If it was gone, we would be trapped onboard. Please let it be that the horses are also still where we tied their reins or it would be a long walk back to Joseph's farm.

Once more we saw the skeletal crew. As they did before, the crew made no effort to stop us. I hoped that it would remain that way until we left. Soon Joseph and I came to where we first boarded and looking down I breathed a sigh of relief. So did Joseph. The ladder was still there. Joseph went down it first as I stood watch with my rifle. Once he was halfway down, I followed.

We jumped off the ladder's lowest rungs onto the riverbank. The horses were still there. We untied them, mounted, and rode away from the ship at good speed.

The cold January wind hit us on the way up from the river. From behind us, we heard a noise. Joseph and I halted the horses and turned them around. The sails on the ship were being moved by the wind. This time, though, the ship moved, sliding off the riverbank. Before our eyes, it reversed course. We watched it sail off with the coffin and its crew of walking skeletons. Then it disappeared.

Joseph turned his horse back around. It was clear he wanted to leave the river. The wind hit us hard as we rode back to his farmhouse. During the several hours it took us to reach his farmhouse we did not speak of what we saw on the ship.

That night I dinned with Joseph and his family. Also dining with us were his field hands. They also lived in the farmhouse and Joseph and Sharon treated them as family. At dinner, neither Joseph nor I spoke of the terrible ship we saw earlier that day or of the unsettling discoveries of the skeleton crew and the coffin.

That night, I retired shortly after the evening meal. It was the last time I ever saw my friend alive.

The next morning Joseph never came down to breakfast. Sharon went up to their bedroom. She found him lying in their bed, his eyes closed. She jostled Joseph's body but he did not move. Sharon spoke to him. He did not respond. Sharon tried to wake him. Joseph did not wake. She saw then that her husband was not breathing. At once, Sharon took action.

The word was passed to one of their field hands to fetch Doctor Sullivan. He lived close to their farm in Bessemer Bend and farmed in addition to operating his medical practice. Doctor Sullivan rode over as fast as he could. He examined Joseph and pronounced him dead. Joseph died sometime in the night, the doctor explained. It seemed to have been a massive heart attack. Doctor Sullivan blamed how hard Joseph over-worked himself on the farm and Sharon believed him. So to did Joseph's children and all of his field hands.

But I knew better. None of them, including Doctor Sullivan, were with Joseph and me when we investigated the ship. They did not know of the coffin in which Joseph saw his own body.

My family arrived at the church. Joseph's family was already inside. My old friend's body was in the wooden coffin made by his loyal field hands. Now, I have come to my decision: I will not tell them or any living soul of the discoveries Joseph and I made on the ship the day before he died.

Sharon and her children would not believe the tale that I have reflected upon during this walk to the church. In addition, I doubt any would believe me, if I dared to tell them, of the terrible discoveries made on that ship by Joseph and me. As for that ship, it is my deepest wish that it never comes ashore ever again. For if any living soul, myself included, ever encounters that ship then they may not only encounter its crew of skeletons but they may, too, find the coffin. And inside of it, if dare they look within, they will find their own body... foretelling their own death.

fEBRUARY

Lincoln's Dagger
D.L. Fowler

Lincoln sat in bed, hugging his knees to his chest as Josh Speed snored beside him. Memories ebbed and flowed—she stood out among the town folks of New Salem lined up on the bluff on a hot August day, all eyes on him as he dislodged the flatboat from the submerged grist mill dam on which it was stuck. Mr. Offutt had refused to listen when Lincoln tried to warn him of anomalies in the current.

When he returned to the tiny village, months later, her sky-blue eyes, golden curls, and slim waistline distinguished her from all the other girls he'd known. He laid awake nights in the loft above Mr. Offutt's store where he clerked, imagining his bony fingers entwined in those blonde locks or tracing the lines of her palms. His breath stalled every time she passed the store on her way to her father's grist mill, sashaying along in a floral skirt.

His tongue lost all sense of purpose whenever she stopped in the store to pick up mail. He was crestfallen to learn she had, not just a beau, but a fiancé who traveled east and had not written to her for months. The pain in her eyes stabbed his heart each time he had to say, "Sorry, not today ... but don't lose hope. I'm sure there will be a letter next week." Of course, part of him hoped there wouldn't be.

She finally gave up after two years, and as he had always yearned for, her heart found a new home in his.

For the next year, his fingers not only explored her curls and traced the lines in the palms of her graceful hands, they laced bonds with her fingers and cupped her warm cheeks. Her soft lips brushed his weathered neck and kissed his quivering lips.

Then came the argument and estrangement. After that, the typhus epidemic and nursing the sick and dying consumed her days and nights, until the fever raged in her. She called for him with her dying breaths, and he sat with her until the end.

Three years since her passing, the melody of her voice haunted him when he recalled her favorite poets. Her wit and logic possessed him every time he stood to debate in the legislature. Her father liked to boast, "Annie and Abraham are the best students our debating school has ever seen."

Night deepened in the loft above the general store, erasing shadows in the bedroom he shared with Speed. Lincoln grasped for the hem of sleep just outside his reach ... desperate for refuge from his thoughts.

He rose. Climbed down the ladder. Padded barefoot, almost floated across the floorboards, not making the slightest creak. The door opened as if anticipating his presence. He proceeded into the street.

All of Springfield, Illinois, was quiet.

If he were asked, he could not tell how he found himself past midnight, some twenty miles away from the store, on an open field at the edge of the nearly abandoned village of New Salem, with no awareness of time passing. A lonely hooting owl let out a moan, echoing Lincoln's agony as he trembled on his knees beside Annie's grave, fearful of the approaching storm. The air around him chilled at an alarming rate. Rain fell in sheets, pelting his shoulders, pasting his soaked shirt to his back. Tears streamed down his face, distinguishable only by their saltiness compared to the storm's virginal dousing. He prostrated himself on freshly turned sod mounded over her coffin, desperate to hold her remains from washing away as ground waters swelled, inundated the grassland, and joined the overflow of flooding rivers and streams.

Were she a seed planted in the ground, nurtured by gentle rains and sunshine, rather than a corpse moldering in a grave, she would sprout, and become again the beautiful flower she once was. He could hold her. She would bring a smile to his face. How he wished he might smile again. *Smile again? I laugh and smile only to ease my pain ... to escape a world where I am damned to never know pleasure ... to never hope.*

A flash of lightning, an explosion of thunder, blackness and silence fell like a shroud around him. Then came a woosh of wind, the slap of waves on a boat's hull. The boat dipped and fell, dipped and fell through swells and troughs of sea... faster and faster... the sea billowing higher around him.

The boat climbed the back of a sea crest so high it might launch him to the moon... or higher... beyond the stars... to paradise... and Annie for all eternity. *Hope can be intoxicating.*

The boat peaked... dove... turned full circle... spun... spun faster... plunged harder... leveled... sailed without a wisp of wind to the cusp of a vast fiery pit. Frightful screams bellowed from the flames. Out of the cacophony a voice cackled, "Welcome to Hell."

"Hell. What is hell to one like me?" Lincoln called out.

"It is the fate of the hopeless," the voice replied. "Listen carefully to the sound of relentless, piercing pain. Endless misery awaits if you carry through with the dark scheme festering in your heart."

"The screams and the pain will help me forget my sorrow," Lincoln replied. "The act shall be done... the steel I carry... I shall thrust it through my heart. Though in Hell, I'll rue it, at least my power to think shall be erased and I will be freed from the hell of earth."

"Once you enter this place, there is no way of escape."

"I have no fear of Hell. I shall take a headlong leap from its highest brink and wallow in its waves."

"Go," the voice said. "Do the deed in the place you've chosen, and I shall prepare a place for you to languish on your return."

Hell erupted in laughter as Lincoln sailed off.

He stood at Annie's graveside an instant later, his hand on the hilt of his dagger nested in its sheath.

His lips trembled as he whispered, "Sweet glistening steel, come forth to speak your powers." He swallowed a lump in his throat. "Rip up the organs of my breath ... and raw my blood in showers."

The dagger slid out of the sheath, as if on its own power. His eyes widened as he gazed at the dagger gripped in his own hand, a glint of moonlight dancing on its finely tuned edge as he held it high, its point aimed at his chest.

The words slid off his tongue against his will. "Strike!"

His heart tremored. His hand quivered. He drew a deep breath to steel his nerves and braced himself. Both hands clasped the hilt. He closed his eyes and plunged the dagger into his chest.

"My last ... my only friend," he murmured as he withdrew the bloody dart and kissed it.

His body convulsed as if he were caught in a thresher. A voice echoed as from a long distance, becoming closer, louder, clearer. "Lincoln," it said.

He knew that voice. "Speed?"

"Lincoln, wake up."

Lincoln sputtered. "I have just had the worst dream."

"What about?"

"It was so real. I visited Annie's grave."

"You do that often."

"I sailed on a ship... crossed the ocean to Hell."

"To Hell?" Speed said. "That cannot be true. The way you describe her, Paradise was created for angels like her."

Lincoln sat up and his body began shaking. "No. She wasn't there. The devil is preparing a place for me."

"It was only a dream," Speed replied.

"But I killed... myself."

"No. We cannot die in our own dreams. You're here. Alive. Safe and sound."

"But suicide is a mortal sin, and I have thought about it," Lincoln said. "I even wrote verses about doing the deed."

"You mean that piece in the *Journal* was by you?" Speed chuckled. "You won't go to Hell for writing about suicide."

Lincoln drew his knees to his chest and rock forward and back.

Speed added, "Of course, you might go to Hell for some of your political speeches."

Lincoln sat up straight. "What if it was a premonition?"

"If that worries you, I can take your pocketknife... but it's been three years since she died. Don't you think it's time you moved on? Sample some of the living fruit life has to offer.?"

"The knife is a good idea." Lincoln gestured to a wooden chair in a corner of the bedroom. "It's in my trouser pocket."

Speed crossed over to the chair and retrieved the

pocketknife. "What about the moving on part?"

"I'm not so comfortable around girls. I always stumble over my words. Can't come up with anything to impress them."

"Sounds like you did well with Annie... before."

"She was one of a kind. We could talk about Euclid... surveying... poets like Burns. She even had opinions on politics. You know, I gave her my grammar book. Even wrote an inscription in it. There are no girls around Springfield who take an interest in things I can talk about."

"Maybe..." Speed hesitated. "Maybe I can introduce you around."

"I don't think you know the types of girls I'm talking about."

Lincoln's new law partner, John Todd Stuart, coaxed him to tag along to a party in Jacksonville more than a year after the suicide poem appeared in the *Sangamon Journal*. During the ball, Stuart introduced Lincoln to his cousin, nineteen-year-old Mary Todd who had recently moved to Springfield after being chased out of her father's house by a difficult stepmother. Short, at five-foot-two-inches, and compact, Stuart's cousin was the opposite of Annie in every way except in intelligence and wit. After dancing with her, Lincoln apologized for his clumsiness. Miss Todd assured him that he was indeed clumsy, but added that she had survived the ordeal, nonetheless.

While traveling back to Springfield from the dance, Mary Todd confided in a friend that she believed she had met the man who would someday help her become Mrs. President. Weeks later, she sat in the front row at a political meeting at which Lincoln delivered an address and approached him afterwards to offer a compliment—she told him he was a better speechmaker than he was a dancer.

Mary's courtship of Lincoln succeeded to the point that they were engaged within a year, though Lincoln broke off the engagement after Mary's younger, more attractive cousin paid a visit to Springfield and turned his head.

Mary's wounded ego healed after a short time, leaving no scars, and she began flitting around town on the arm of Lincoln's archrival, Stephen A. Douglass. She added fuel to the fire by publishing a poetic piece in the *Sangamon Journal* that imitated Lincoln's celebrated biting satire. The butt of the joke was the Illinois State Auditor, James Shields—one of Lincoln's foremost detractors, whom he had skewered in a previously published anonymous lampoon in the same poetic style.

Shields became convinced that Lincoln had written the offensive story and demanded an apology. Lincoln refused to apologize for something he did not do, but on discovering Mary had authored the piece, he accepted responsibility. Shields remained unsatisfied and challenged Lincoln to a duel. Still unwilling to incriminate Mary, Lincoln agreed to the duel, though he insisted on setting the terms of engagement—broadswords, an island in the river, a confined space with bounds that maximized his own unique physical advantages of height and reach.

On the day of the duel, Lincoln insisted on a slight demonstration which proved Shields could not survive the encounter. Both sides agreed to call the contest a draw.

The aborted duel, in fact, gave Mary the upper hand. She owed Lincoln a debt of gratitude, which she satisfied by insinuating herself, without forewarning her gallant defender, into a private dinner at the home of the *Sangamon Journal's* editor and his wife. She apologized profusely to Lincoln for drawing him into danger and showered him with praise for his chivalry—a compliment which he was unaccustomed to receiving. At the conclusion of dinner, all were agreed that Mary and Lincoln should resume their courtship outside of public view—the editor and his wife offered their home for that purpose.

As the courtship progressed in the privacy of the editor's home, Mary coached her intended in the passionate arts. After one particularly amorous evening, Mary insisted they must marry as soon as a local minister could be arranged. Lincoln agreed to make the necessary arrangements, and Mary directed him to call on the Presbyterian minister... the next morning... during breakfast before the parson set about his parish duties.

"When shall the affair take place?" Lincoln asked, "and when?"

"The afternoon," she replied.

"Which afternoon?" Lincoln said.

"Tomorrow," she replied.

"What if he isn't available?"

"The next day, then."

"If that is what you want. I assume we shall do it at the church," he said.

"That or the parsonage, whichever is available."

As it happened, Mary had to iron out a few wrinkles, so the wedding was delayed—briefly. Even though the minister was available at the time Mary had preferred, her sister, Liz, wanted the ceremony conducted in her home. However, Liz refused to cancel her weekly sewing circle scheduled for the same afternoon.

Lincoln took advantage of the delay to purchase rings and the jeweler was able to engrave them.

Following their wedding, Mary and Abraham Lincoln made

their first home in an apartment in Springfield above the Globe Tavern. Their first son, Robert Todd Lincoln, was born nine months later, after which they moved to a modest house at 413 S. Eighth Street in the same city.

They lived in Springfield until moving to Washington for Lincoln's term as president.

Over twenty-two years, five months, and ten days of marriage, it cannot be said that they lived happily thereafter—at least not all of the time.

Not when she clocked him on the bridge of his nose with a log... nor when she chased him out of the house wielding a butcher knife, or a broom, or a pot of scalding water... nor when she criticized him publicly for poor spelling... nor when she scolded him for wearing black gloves instead of white ones to the opera... nor when she hid his trousers to keep him from a Cabinet meeting unless he promised to appoint one of her friends to a plum government job... to name a few.

The Suicide Soliloquy

unattributed

believed to be written by Abraham Lincoln

Here, where the lonely hooting owl
Sends forth his midnight moans,
Fierce wolves shall o'er my carcase growl,
Or buzzards pick my bones.

No fellow-man shall learn my fate,
Or where my ashes lie;
Unless by beasts drawn round their bait,
Or by the ravens' cry.

Yes! I've resolved the deed to do,
And this the place to do it:
This heart I'll rush a dagger through,
Though I in hell should rue it!

Hell! What is hell to one like me
Who pleasures never know;
By friends consigned to misery,
By hope deserted too?

To ease me of this power to think,
That through my bosom raves,
I'll headlong leap from hell's high brink,
And wallow in its waves.

Though devils yell, and burning chains
May waken long regret;
Their frightful screams, and piercing pains,
Will help me to forget.

Yes! I'm prepared, through endless night,
To take that fiery berth!
Think not with tales of hell to fright
Me, who am damn'd on earth!

Sweet steel! come forth from your sheath,
And glist'ning, speak your powers;
Rip up the organs of my breath,
And draw my blood in showers!

I strike! It quivers in that heart
Which drives me to this end;
I draw and kiss the bloody dart,
My last—my only friend!

"Lincoln's Dagger" is based on the poem "The Suicide Soliloquy," unattributed and published 1838 in the Sangamon Journal, and believed to have been written by Abraham Lincoln on the third anniversary of Anne Rutledge's death.

MARCH

How to Survive the Dark
Joe Nasta

1. Don't Use the Toilet

Sheila went down to the creek alone, although it was already dark. She'd used the bathroom with no water during the power outage – while the unflushed idea of scampering through the dark with an overflowing bucket to fill the toilet tank made her shudder, the thought of the guy she'd met on Lex unwittingly opening the toilet seat lid to the stench gave her heart palpitations. The decision came easily to squeeze into her boots sockless, wiggle into her maroon Patagonia puffy, and sneak away without telling Benji. He was tending the fireplace in the guest suite of the house.

It would only take a minute, she thought. He wouldn't even notice she'd been gone.

"A Subaru! I actually don't know how to drive," Sheila said on their third date at Machiavelli's last month. Benji stared out the window at the lit upper floor apartments across the street. She cleared her throat. He still didn't turn back towards her. She returned to linguini after a sip of sauvignon blanc, beginning to feel

neglected for the first time since they'd met.

"But would you like to give me a ride to my friend's home up north? I'm housesitting in a few weeks at the start of March." His eyes darted towards her, then back across the street.

They sat at the best seat in the cozy Italian restaurant. There were only two other occupied tables since it was nearing closing time. They'd waited longer than necessary for this, the perfect table for the perfect date, and flirted over drinks at the small wooden bar while the other tables emptied – he drank a gin martini while she preferred a dirty Shirley. He knew the hostess, who knew exactly where he wanted to sit and laughed about all the different friends he'd sat across from over the past year.

"And hardly ever a repeat guest! You must have a lot of friends," she said knowingly, glancing at Sheila only from the corner of her eye.

His laugh struck glass as he pulled the chair out for her to sit. It became clear why he enjoyed this table in particular when he spent the entire meal gazing out at the pedestrians bumbling in the rain towards the bars up Pine Street.

"I like to people watch, sorry," Benji shook his head jerkily, then made direct eye contact with a sideways smile. Something was different tonight.

He was broodingly handsome, charming, and said very nice things to her when they were alone in the bedroom. Sheila felt comfortable when the tops of his cheeks rose or his black eyebrows arched. Maybe it was relaxed shoulders or attentive gaze, the small face movements when she talked or cool confidence but something tonight was missing.

The candles on the table were almost completely melted into pools of hot wax. When he said yes, he would love to take her up to the house in the woods the first Friday in March, she leaned *back in her chair and finally relaxed. He'd already finished eating, but looked hungrily towards her. "But let's pay and get out of here," a playful note in his voice reminded her why she liked spending time with him.*

Now, stranded in the cold, dark house with Benji, she was grateful he was there to tend the fire. It was comforting not to be alone. Just as she reached the trail's entrance at the edge of the woods, Sheila realized that she'd forgotten the flashlight on the bathroom counter.

2. Never Go Alone

The rock in the middle of the creek. The water flowing around it. Continuing, continuing. The only way to reach it to wade, the water rising towards her ankles, feet soaking through the seams of the boots as the wet poured over. The night sky, threads of light pulled Sheila towards the rock.

She wanted to move towards something and to reach it, then stand still for a while. Deep in the center of her hips she longed for a single moment in the rain that meant something deeper, that transformed the terrible night into one worth moving through. Sheila slid her feet along the rocks under the water, sliding forward.

The bucket dropped. A whistle.

3. Don't Let the Fire Go Out

Benji was no good at starting the fire.

Sheila sat on the love seat across from the fireplace grate holding a flashlight, a flannel and fleece blanket wrapped tightly around her shoulders. "Brrr," she shivered and the light shifted to the left and right of where he was trying to see. The wind whisked above the hot tub just outside the glass French doors, under which the seal was tearing off.

As the bright beam moved, bits of char and particulates in the air shimmered. Under typical light, the sun illuminated natural. The electric lamps next to the recliner washed the room, but in the dark a different layer of filth emerged, perhaps imagined, into a smoke plume in the soft yellow.

His form crouched around the small pile of torn-up Trader Joe's bag he found in the pantry, used for kindling. His hand reached blindly behind his left Chuck Taylor for the long-barreled lighter's red handle. He squinted at the ash, pulled the trigger.

Click, hiss. Orange light and the kindling burst. Her voice again, "And now the smaller pieces, but don't starve it." Sheila's grip shifted and so did the light. To the left of the hearth were the thick logs, and to the right splintered sections of one inch by one inch wood.

"I'll do my best." Benji laughed and rolled his eyes. *What the hell was he doing here again?*

"Well, I'm going to look for more blankets. You're taking too long!" She stuck out her tongue and scurried away before he could respond. The room was darker lit only by the weak flame. Sheila had taken the flashlight with her. The small lapping cracked. It began to catch the wood he'd placed on the crackling tongue, but went out.

Then he only heard the wind.

4. Salvage the Embers

A seed in the ash glinted. He wanted to dig into the soot. As his fingers burrowed into the grey pile under the unburnt pieces of wood, he inhaled. He hoped it wasn't too late to rekindle as the scraps of char weighed into both of his palms, under his nails.

He sat in the dark by himself for a minute or two before he started to wonder where she had gone. Was that a door slam? He couldn't see anything because his eyes had not yet adjusted. It wasn't that he was afraid. Benji missed the sharp edges of Sheila's voice and the quick movements of her head as she watched everything around her at once, her thin lips pressing into a smile. Another moment passed.

A hinge creaked, footsteps. The empty room turned to grey. Nobody returned.

5. Don't Panic

He waited in the dark by the dead fire.

The Aquarium was busy on their first date.

A shiver, a moan.

"What kind of fish would you be?" he asked, trying to stop from smiling as she shook her shagged brown hair, brushed it out of her face. All around was filled with the hallow sound bouncing between the tanks and refracted light rippled over the vine of flowers tattooed on her arm. Benji motioned towards the tank's placard with an array of species illustrated, explained.

"Me? I'm not in this one—"

Grabbed his left wrist and pulled, glided quickly between the families standing still with wide eyes glued to the glass.

Sheila brought him to the sting ray pool and plunged her hand in. "This is where I belong," she asserted too brashly. "I mean I'll never sting. I'll even let you touch me," fingerpads on the inside of his forearm, "but then I'll leave."

The rays swam towards them. She let go of him. They both

felt the graceful silk backs under the surface before they sliced metallic towards a woman in a purple blouse.

It was starting to get even colder.

"Me, I'm in there." Benji pointed across to the wall of throbbing jellyfish. The mindless goo pulsed as their tentacles bloomed, threatening venom. *"I will sting and you'll have to piss on me."* He could only keep a straight face for seconds before bursting into a laugh. *"No, I just like the way they glow."* The electric luminescence curled the hairs beginning to burst through his chin, empty coincidences.

Their faces. She didn't want him to blink his green eyes.

He felt embarrassed about the fire, that he couldn't start it.

That's when he saw through the transparent French doors her running in the rain swinging an orange Home Depot bucket.

6. Use a Flashlight

The fat drops hitting water, the pulse of the creek, and the wind roared as Sheila stepped into the cold stream. The rain streaked down her face but her vision had adjusted under the eerie dim moonlight that broke through the clouds as she throbbed forward.

They slept together after their second date. Something about the way that Benji bowled had excited her, how he turned to stick his tongue out at her as he picked up his marbled orange ball from the return carousel and set his fingers just right before attempting the approach. Three quick steps under the ultraviolet light before his hand twisted, released the ball sideways down the alley and his right foot hooked behind the other. Ugh. The way he cheered when the pins fell, the veins in his biceps, and hair on his forearms swelled her chest with joy.

There was a cool ache behind her sternum that sped up her throat and the back of her mouth. If only she could make it to the rock to throw her arms wide, soak in the downpour. Take a deep breath. Be alone just for a moment before resuming her pretending. She could be a wanted body. After all, she wanted his. Her feet were completely soaked and the waterline twisted around her middle calves as she waded towards the boulder.

The football game was on a projector screen at the end of the alley, but she kept her focus on the white pins when it was her turn to bowl. She'd accidentally gotten her shoes half a size too big so she stepped decisively and slowly towards the beginning of the run, too rigid. As soon as the ball left her fingers Sheila knew it was a wasted shot – straight into the gutter. It made her angry but instead she turned around, lit up her face, and laughed. Benji came to her, grabbed her hips, and kissed her for the first time as the guys in the next lane cheered at the Seahawks' touchdown.

She did not laugh now. It wasn't anger that she felt, only an unnameable desire that grew from the innermost parts of her to every corner of her being as she high-stepped onto stone.

7. Stay Inside

Sheila was in the middle of the creek standing on a rock, looking up at the sky when Benji made it to the end of the dark trail. The rain was still coming down, hard.

"What are you—" It was too loud to hear each other between the overflow rush of the water, which effectively cut her off. The crown of her head rose towards the sky and he reticently stepped into the stream to inch closer towards her rooted on the boulder.

"I noticed you were gone. I wanted—" What could he possibly want from her? They barely knew each other yet. But still they reached towards each other as the air began to hum with a yellow intensity as the wind brought a burning smell.

Crack. A whir. The thick trunk of a tree smacking sand, water with a splash. The lights from the house clicked on, exposing them soaking wet to each other, unsure of what either of them would say next.

aPRIL

The Peakingas
Dakoda Foxx

On a warm April morning, in a small town called The Char, Dan Peakingas sat out front on his porch, sipping a cup of coffee. The sun was shining so bright, he sat with his summer shades on.

His neighbor came out to water his lawn. Dan tried to go unnoticed and made no eye contact. He hoped his neighbor wouldn't come over. Trying to keep conversation short, he said, "Top of the morning," as he smiled and waved. "Just trying to enjoy a quick cup of coffee before going in," he added.

Every year the neighbor came over and played a joke on him. Today was Dan's birthday. He was normally grumpy on this day because everyone always wanted to make jokes and try to fool him. Today was April Fool's Day. Dan usually tried to avoid people all day each year, but it never worked.

His friends always took him somewhere and fooled him. So, he was getting himself prepared for this. Today should be just an ordinary day: hanging with his friends, and they play a small joke one him... so he thought.

It started off with a bang but turned into something much more.

Paul called me on three-way and said, "Hey, Jon. Dan is on the phone."

Dan yelled, "I want to go to Reed for my birthday today, to the Byron Show. Would you drive us, Jon?"

I said, "Okay, who all is going?"

Paul said, "Me, you, Dan, Max, and Cody—if we can find him."

"Okay, I'm down. Let's do this, " I said. "I have to pack. What time are we leaving?"

Dan answered, "Reed is about two hours away so we have to start in an hour in order to get a hotel room and find a good place to set up on the grass for the show. It's 12 pm now."

Paul said, "I have to call Max and Cody. I will call you both back when I am ready. I am excited! The Byron Show is going to be lit. Okay, y'all—talk to you soon."

Paul called Max and said, "Man, Dan wants to go to the Byron Show tonight. Pack up—and Jon is driving, so you can relax and have fun."

Max said, "Okay, cool. I will be ready, just come by and get me. I can't wait to play an April Fool's joke on Dan. I got a good one this year."

Paul said, "Max, you know Dan don't like those April Fool's jokes played on him."

"Never mind that, Paul. You'll like it for sure. I will do it when I get to the hotel up there."

Paul said, "He will be so mad."

Max said, "I know, but he will be okay."

Then Paul called Cody. Cody was a lady's man and he had two ladies right there while he was on the phone. Paul said, "Are you listening, man? We are going to Reed to the Byron Show for Dan's birthday. Come up for air for a moment and go with us. Jon is driving so you can drink. I am buying a few cases of beer, man, so what you say?"

Cody said, "Well, just for tonight, right? My girls can stay here till I get back. Count me in—I will be waiting for y'all to come get me."

Dan met me outside with his suitcase and looked up at the sky and smiled real big. He said, "The sky looks great and the sun is shining bright. Can't wait to get to the show tonight. Hopefully the moon and the stars are just as bright."

I said, "I am sure they will."

We picked up Paul and went to the store to get beer and snacks. Then we went to pick up Max and Cody.

Of course, Cody had a long, drawn-out goodbye with his ladies. One of them was crying and saying, "Can't wait till you get back!"

He said, "It's just overnight, my loves. I will be back."

As we drove into Reed, we saw lots of stuff—like the Blowfish Kettle Restaurant and the Reed grocery store. But by then it was 3 pm and we needed to check in at the hotel. Of course, Cody wanted to stop at the Blowfish Kettle before the hotel, but Dan insisted they get their rooms first and then come back.

I couldn't believe my eyes. I just couldn't turn away—it was like I was stuck, with nowhere to go but this lone rustic old diner called 'Come Out'. It looked like something from the fifties—but this was 2019 and not your ordinary diner.

As I drove up to park, people stopped to stare at us. There was one woman that was staring so hard she went into a building then ran out to the next one. This felt strange, but Max was like, "Maybe they never seen city folks before... or in a long time?"

Dan and the others got out of the car and headed towards the hotel, which was a block and a half away. He was going to check them in for the night, and I was going to park.

Dan and the gang got to the hotel reception desk to check in and the lady at the desk said, "How may I help you?" just as I came running in all out of breath, waving my hands, asking, "Hey, do you have valet parking or do you park yourself? We parked down the block."

She said, "You can park yourself free of charge in our garage if you stay with us—just place the parking pass on the dash. Or you can use the valet and we will park you for $35 a night and additional five dollar convenience fee."

I was like, "No, thank you. I will park myself, thank you."

We all got a room on the fifth floor. We got our stuff from the car and took it to our rooms and set to meet at the Blowfish Restaurant. Whoever got to the restaurant first would get a booth for the five of them.

Everyone walking down the hall to their rooms and Paul said, "Okay, I have to take a dump, and I'll be down after that. So make sure you save me a spot—and Cody dont pick up any women while you're there!"

Paul's room was just off the elevator to the left—room 501—and my room was right down the hall, in room 513. Max and Cody was down the hall and on the right of the elevator, in rooms 514 and 518.

Paul got to his room and a man across the hall in room 525 was standing there. He was leaning on the door crooked, with a straw in his mouth. He had this weird grin on his face. He had a can of chips, dangling them at Paul. He said with this weird voice, "Hey, mate, you want some?"

Paul said, "No, no, thank you."

The man said, "You don't want to miss the show tonight," again asking, "You're sure you don't want any chips mate?" and made this loud chuckle.

Paul pushed open the door and rushed in without looking back. Jon watched him go in like an alley cat chasing a rat.

Dan got to his and went in, and Jon watched him shut the door.

What happened next was very unexpected.

I came down to the lobby and Max met up with me by the door. He said, "Cody should be coming along soon. Let's start walking over to the place."

As we were walking, I keep hearing my name being called. From the distance, I saw this woman in the shadows calling, "Jon."

Well, I turned around to see who it was and kept walking because I didn't know the woman. But my name was being called louder and louder.

Then I heard footsteps coming abruptly behind me and as I turned around someone jumped on my back. I was startled by this, flapping my hands and running around and I finally heard her say, "Stop, you fool, it's me, Megan!"

Almost hitting her and running, I turned to look at her and said, "Why are you jumping on me and Max, and scaring the hell out of me in this creepy town?!"

She was like, "You're not listening to me." Then Megan disappeared.

I looked confused at Cody who had just joined us. Cody

said, "Bro, what's the weird look for?"

Max said, "Well, this woman named Megan came up to us." When Cody looked confused, he added, "Didn't you see a woman standing there?"

"What woman?" Cody looked around and didn't see anyone. "Wow, you guys already started drinking without me?"

I yelled, "We should be going now!"

Max said, "Let's head to the Blowfish Restaurant. Let's just go and eat good food and forget this. Have great drinks at the bar and then go to the Byron Show for our night life."

Cody agreed. He wanted to sow his oats before he got back to his ladies.

Dan got to the restaurant first. He was scared and shaking, sitting in a booth, sipping a soda.

"It looks creepy," said Cody as we got to the big table by the window where Dan was sitting. This window was so big that it took up the whole wall.

As Max sat down at the table and looked over the drink menu that was on the table, he said, "Go ahead, Jon, tell them about your new girlfriend."

I said, "She's not my girlfriend. And I never met her ever."

Max said, "Well, she sure do know you," then changed the subject. "Call Paul, let's see where he is at."

Dan called Paul but it didn't go though. There was no signal at all.

I was just about to get up and go to the bathroom when the waitress came to the table. I looked up with a big gulp. She had a black apron dusty with flour, with these black jeans that looked a bit too tight and a shirt that showed her ample cleavage.

She said, "Hi, my name is Betty and I will be your server

tonight." Looking at us, she asked, "Oh, yeah. You those boys from The Char, and you're here for Dan's birthday, right? Happy birthday, Dan!"

Dan said, "Thank you! How did you know who we were and my name?"

Betty said, "Are you looking for your friend Paul? The other waitress said he was here first, in that booth. She went to get another customer's order and then he was gone."

Everyone ordered, and we were sitting and talking about what we were going to do tonight. The people in the restaurant was looking at us as we ate. We couldn't help but to notice what the people next to us was doing. They were eating but then putting food in their bags to go. The people that was next to them at the table ran out the diner with the whole plate.

The waitress sighed and the cook said, "This is the third time this week. They didn't pay again."

"I have to call the police again," the waitress said.

Everyone was here, but still not Paul yet. We tried to call but none of our phones worked. Dan looked at the waitress and said, "We know she knows something."

I said, "She's walking funny, look."

Cody said, "Normally, I would think that was sexy but that's downright scary. She walked like she was swinging on a pole and shaking."

Max said, "She looks like the girl from Exorcist."

Then the waitress turned around at the door and said, "Orders in!" and glowed bright then exploded all over the place, sending little red orbs everywhere.

"Why did we even picked this place?" Dan asked. He seemed freaked out but assumed it was somehow part of an elaborate prank. I knew better.

"How can this be happening?" I ran out of the restaurant and tried to leave but ended back inside the restaurant. "What?!"

"Well, I have to pee," Max said, half in shock, and was halfway stood up when there was a loud *bump* in the back and everyone in the restaurant looked. Max turned back to look at us like *heck no...*

We weren't alone—there were more people in the restaurant as well. All of them was scared. Paul was normally our level-headed person but he was still not here yet.

There was an old couple sitting at the bar who had been reading the newspaper and drinking coffee. Then there was a group of four guys at a table celebrating a bachelor's party. They were being a little loud earlier but now they were scared and talking fast and shaking. One of them was in the corner freaking out, yelling, "We're all going to die!"

One of the other men went up to him and smacked him so hard, yelling at him, "Stop it, Tyler, just stop it!"

The cook was in front, on the phone, trying to call the police... but there was no answer. The cook said, "No dial tone. Does anyone have a dial tone? Can anyone call out?"

Megan came in the restaurant and said, "What are you bitches doing?"

Dan yelled, "Jon, Jon, *Jon!*"

I turned so fast in a dazed and cleared my throat and said, "*What?!*"

There was a spider—a big one, dangling from the light fixture on the wall. My eyes got huge and I was crawling across the table to get away from it. I yelled, "Someone get it, get it away from me before it give me a heart attack! Or gets me!"

Max grabbed it and took it to the door and let it go.

"Now I got to worry about the spider jumping on me

when I leave," I told him, still freaked out. "Why didn't you kill it?"

Max said, "*Dude*, no! You have things to worry about other than a spider *right now!*"

I said, "Yes: the spider, Paul missing, that woman Megan who keeps calling my name, and exploding Betty over there. Yes, I know!"

We looked around to see where Megan was at. She had disappeared. We were all confused—she was just here calling my name again. Where was she? I know she couldn't just vanish in thin air.

Dan says, "Cody, is this your April fool's joke? Ha ha ha you win," he added nervously.

Cody said, "It's not me. Naw, really, it is not me this time."

Dan said, "You have girls all over. Thought that Megan was one of your girls. Shoot, you're always fooling around."

The boys from the back group was getting louder and one got up. He walked over to the cook and said, "Aren't you going to see what happened to Betty?"

The cook said, "Uh, no, you go see. I will keep trying to call for help."

Two women tried to leave the restaurant but couldn't. One of the women yelled, "Sara, we can't leave! What are we going to do?"

The group of guys tried to go out and couldn't. The one guy said, "We seen you go out and take the spider. Go try again."

Max got up and went to the door. He stood there for a moment and before pushing the door, he said to Sara, "You try first." Sara pushed the door but it wouldn't budge. Max said, "Okay, let me try." He pushed open the door and went outside.

Sara tried but it was like something was blocking her from leaving the restaurant. One of the other men who called himself

Rick went to the door and pushed the door open and went out. As both of them look back at the restaurant, they saw that the others couldn't come outdoors. It was puzzling to them. They both came back inside and sat down, looking confused.

"We have to find out what is keeping us here and why won't it let most of us leave this restaurant," I said aloud. "Someone has to go to see where Paul is. Maybe he is in his hotel room? Max, will you check?"

Max left but quickly came back and said that he couldn't find Paul. He wasn't at the hotel and he didn't check out yet according to the lady at the front desk. Max mentioned that the lady at the hotel was acting weird like she was in a trance or something, rocking back and forth with a wide grin on her face. "It was really weird," Max finished.

The police came in after all of that. An officer came to the table and asked, "Is there anything I can help you with?"

I said, rambling in a bit of a panic, "Yes, my friend Paul is missing, and he was supposed to come to the restaurant with us after we checked in at the hotel but her never made it, so can we file a missing person report?"

The officer told us that we must wait twenty-four hours before we could make an official missing person report.

"What about the waitress that exploded?" Max asked.

Another officer called, "I will request backup." She looked around and seen that there were animals running around in the restaurant and outside like crazy. She said, "Did you notice all the animals?" as she headed to the front door.

Max opened the door for the officer. She told them she would be back shortly, walked out the door, and exploded. This bright red orb came from her. It was all around then disappeared.

Everyone started yelling and screaming.

Megan appeared and said, "This is not good." Then she was gone again.

Dan walked over to the window, staring at the animals. With his hands on his head, he looked amazed, saying, "She's right, look, she's right! How come we didn't realize this? Look, everyone! Oh my God, there's so many cats and dogs running around out. What is going on? Why are there so many animals out there running around?"

Cody remembered that there was a tug on his leg, but he didn't know what it was. He looked down and he didn't see anything. When he looked up there was a rat sitting over there in a corner moving his arms up and down in a circle motion.

Max notice the rat but he said, "Oh, this place is from the fifties, so it could have all kinds of infestations."

Dan said, "That was good to know! You should have told us that you saw a rat, we would have definitely not ordered here."

Max said, "Do you not know how many places we go to that have rodents and different things in them and we still eat there?" He shook his head and said, "Never mind that. Do you not see that there's a plethora of cats and dogs outside? They're not like ordinary cats and dogs running around—they're running around like they have lost something or are on a mission... or like there's something out there that's chasing them."

Cody jumped on the table like he was surfing and said, "Yes, they're on a mission to find all the girls and take them from me!" He yelled at the window, "Hey you animals, save some girls for me! I haven't got out there yet. Stop acting like an animal— save some for me!" He fell to the floor yelling, "Please!" with his hands over his head.

Dan said, "I'm not going to eat anything in here anymore because of the rat. I do not think you understand. This is not the way I want to eat or the night I want on my birthday. Not with exploding Betty over there, or the exploding police woman—that's not a good thing!"

Max said, "I do not know what's going on but I do know that I am tired, I'm scared, and I want to get out of here."

Dan said, "I want to drink lots of drinks and have a little fun! I didn't come all this way to sit here and talk about exploding Betty and the cats and dogs that are running around like they're crazy outside. Well, guys, I guess this is anytime better than now to tell you what I saw in my room when I went in there. I wasn't going to tell y'all until later on... when I asked to come and sleep in somebody else's room."

Max said, "What did you see, what did you see?"

Dan said, "I saw everything that was supposed to be on the ground level on the ceiling—my bed was on the ceiling, my dresser was on the ceiling, the TV was on the ceiling, the lamp and everything was on the ceiling. The only thing that was on floor level was the light. When I flipped the switch for the light, the chandelier was standing at attention up on the floor, lit up. I didn't know what to do—the bathroom was upside down, as well. I took one look and said, 'Oh no,' and ran out. I didn't know what else to do. I thought maybe that somebody was trying to play an April Fool's joke on me and that's what it could be. I thought maybe Max or Cody was trying to play a prank on me and I did not like it."

"Oh no," Max said, "I did tell Paul that I was going to play a trick on you when we got here to the hotel, but I was not going to do *that!* That was not me at all. Since we got here things have been different and very weird. I can't understand what's happening and I don't know what we should do because everything is weird and keeps changing on us."

Cody said, "I don't know if y'all notice or not, but we had exploding Betty, missing Paul, an unknown girl who keeps calling Jon's name, we can't leave the restaurant,, animals running around like rapid outside, Dan's room is upside down, there was a man at 507 standing outside his door waiting for Paul, and a rat in the corner that keeps waving and flopping his hands—no, not at all strange. Do you not understand what is happening?"

I said, "I understand what's happening, I just don't know what to do about it. We'll just have to figure out something and try to find Paul. This is weird for even him because he's normally the one that would beat us here and the level-headed one so for him to be gone is really racking my brain right now. Even if we found him there's no way out of this restaurant—the only one that can leave is Max. Why is Max the only one that can leave and come back? He went to the hotel to look for Paul and came back. He took the spider outside and then came back. Now we have to figure out how the rest of us can get out and go back to the hotel."

In just that moment we heard a loud *bump* again, like we did before, but this time it was louder. Everyone looked and turned towards the kitchen. Last time, Betty exploded when we heard that *bump.*

There it was—the big bright red glow and then we heard *bloop,* followed by a loud *bang* that sounded like pots dropping.

The old guy asked, "One of you guys going to go back there and see what that was? Me and Martha, we cannot go back there. We're too old to defend ourselves. We have to send one of you younger guys so you can fight them off for us and see what's happening."

Max said, "Well, I'm not going—because I'm the youngest... I think. And I wouldn't know what to do or what to look for at all. See, I was learning from Cody how to be a ladies' man—not a hit man."

The guy from earlier, Rick, said, "I'll go see what it is—don't worry."

Dan said, "Thank you, thank you, sir. We appreciate you going for us—we are all just scared."

The man said, "It's okay. We are all scared here, but I know someone has to go and see what's happening."

At that moment one of the man's friends called, "Rick! Rick, get a weapon!"

Rick grabbed a broom to push the kitchen door open and grabbed a frying pan. He looked around there was nothing but he heard a rattle coming from the back. Maybe the back door?

Rick walked to the back door and opened it up and could see the hotel. Then he noticed the guy from the hotel running towards them. He pushed through the doors, yelling, "Hurry and shut the door!" He looked afraid and locked it behind him. He was rambling saying, "They look like people... but they are not there, there, there..." And he passed out cold on the floor.

Cody and Dan helped get the man to a booth. "He hit his head really hard. What he was saying?" Cody wondered aloud.

Dan was trying to wake him and asked, "Hey, what's your name? Hey, what happened to you?"

The man woke up growling and yelling, "We have to go! We have to go! My name is Buddy—I work over there at the hotel. There are things going on over there! There are monsters—those people are monsters!" he yelled. "It is crazy over there!"

Dan laughed at his growl and said, "Well, to the monsters, *we* look like monsters. And you sure growl like one."

Rick noticed a cat and a little puppy run out of the kitchen near the freezer. He said, "What in the world?! How did these animals get into the restaurant freezer?!"

Hearing a *pop* and a *sizzle* he looked over at the grill—it was on fire. "Somebody grab a fire extinguisher!" he yelled.

The cook had disappeared and the pots and pans with the food had dropped all on the floor. The stove was on fire, the grill was smoking, and the soup was boiling over on the floor.

Rick said, "I don't know what's happening. This is strange y'all! Now the cook is gone—we just saw him talking to the police! They went in the back and now both of them are gone!"

I said, "This is even stranger than anything that I've ever seen before."

Rick asked, "Is any one of y'all staying at the hotel down the street?" Everyone answered in agreement except the elderly couple—they lived thirty minutes away but were regulars at the diner. "There's something I must show you back at the hotel."

I said, "What floor are you on? Just curious."

He said, "I'm on the fifth floor. Why you asked?"

"I'm in room 509. My friends, too," I told him.

Rick said, "My boys are up there, too. Tyler is in room 511, Josh is in 515, and Asher in 517."

"Don't you find it very strange that we all are on the fifth floor? This can't be no coincidence."

"We have to get out of here," Rick said, nodding. "We have to get to the hotel. We all can try to go thought the back door the way Buddy came out."

We followed Rick to the back door. He opened it and looked out to see if there was a clear path to the hotel. "Everyone ready?"

Max said, "I will hold the door open until everyone is out. Then I will close it behind us just in case we have to run back into here. It won't be locked."

Rick said, "Okay, everyone must stay close. We don't know what's going on out there or what we're up against. Okay, everyone ready? Let's go."

We ran out the door, keeping close behind Rick and quickly found ourselves at the hotel. Inside, we saw four guys at the front desk and as we got closer, I heard them ask the hotel manager for Officer Carl. She told them she had not seen him at all today, then asked if they needed a room. They shook their heads *no*.

Then what happened after that was something unbelievable. Buddy started jumping up and down in fear, pointing to the men, yelling, "Monsters, monsters I tell you—"

I grabbed him and put my hand over his mouth. "Ssshhh, quiet!" I whispered. "You don't want them to come get you? Then be quiet! Shut up or we will leave you here with your monsters!"

Suddenly it went silent but then there was a *click* and the lights went out. I looked around to find a flashlight or some kind of light but just as quickly the room was illuminated and the four men were gone.

Speechless, Max was smacking my arm and Dan was pulling on me hard. That was when I looked at the door... but it was upside down! No, the whole room was upside down. I ran to the door and got out. I ran so fast, and everyone came streaming out behind me.

We all stood in the hallway in disbelief. Finally, Rick said, "Let's go, I still have to show you. It's down the hall here, in the big meeting room."

As we walked, he explained, "We came to celebrate Steve's wedding and was going to rent a meeting room here, but we decided to go to the Byron Show instead." Rick stopped at a door and told us, "Okay, now when I open up this door, you can't make a sound. You have to be quiet." He opened up the door wide and everyone stood, even more shocked.

I whispered, "I have never seen anything like this before…"

In this big meeting room there were people standing around, wall to wall, in a circles with red glowing lights going through their heads. The room was sideways and the center of the circle had slime floating in the middle of it. They held hands and hummed, "*Elpapi Manyanoyo,*" and there were cats and dogs running all around them. Almost everyone in the town was in the room. People were exploding and turning into animals and then the animals were turning into slime. It was chaos.

Rick said quietly, "Whatever this is, it's been going on since yesterday. I don't know how they know my cousin Elpapi… But I don't know anyone name Manyanoyo… Does anyone?"

Max asked, "What was that in the corner?"

We looked and it was the four men who had disappeared from the front desk. They were saying, "*Peakingas… Peakingas…*"

Dan tapped my shoulder, saying, "Let's go. Let's go. Those men look scary and we all should go now."

There was a man running, coming our way, past those men and toward us. He was yelling "*The Peakingas!*"

We all ran to the door, everyone scared, and shut the meeting room doors before the guy got to us. We heard a loud bang on the door and quickly ran back to the lobby.

Rick said, "So *that's* what I saw when I was on my way to the restaurant. I thought it was a show until I saw that same light with the waitress and the cook. Now I know it wasn't a show."

We looked outside and saw all the animals running

around, now understanding that they are the people from the town.

There was a rat again on the hotel desk waving his arms again like at the restaurant and standing up on his back legs. Then the cat from the restaurant came in and the rat ran to Max and went in between his legs.

Dan said, "The rat likes you, Max."

Max looked closer at the rat. It was moving back and forth. Max bent down and picked the rat up and as he brought it up closer to his face, it immediately jumped on Max's shoulder and ran around his neck. Then it went to his ear with a squawking sound.

The cat jumped on the counter and at first it was making the same squawking sound, then it sat by Max's leg. Max said, "I don't know what's going on. These animals are coming to me. What is this?"

We saw another red glowing ball and watched as the big orb came down into the cat and dog and then the dog started running around in circles.

I said, "Is this like the invasion of the body snatchers—but animal snatchers?!"

There were little red orbs all around us. Dan said, "Are those all people? Are we going to be a red orb too?" He started to freak out and yell. "Oh no! We're going to become one of those things!"

"Calm down, Dan! We're going to get out of this. It's your birthday and we can't let you die today!" I reassured him, though I barely believed me.

The rat got off Max's shoulder and nudged his leg. The cat ran in between them. Then we heard, "*Peakingas.*"

Dan said, "Did you hear that?"

Max said, "Yeah, isn't it your name?"

Rick said, "Yeah. I think I heard it back at the hotel meeting room."

Suddenly Megan appeared again, close to Dan. She said to him, "It all starts with you, Dan. You're the key." She turned to me. "I came to warn you. Look, look." She pointed across the street. "I have loved you for many years. My cortex is attached to the orb. I see things and know what's going on. I can't leave but I can help get you and your friends out of here. I want you safe. Then she said, "*Vestmo daminga nananu Manyanoyo,*" and disappeared.

Across the road, where Megan had pointed, was a community center with two small buses. "Maybe we can get out of here with them," I suggested.

Rick said, "Great thinking, Jon. Who knows how to hotwire a bus?"

We all gathered some stuff to take with us. We had food and blankets just in case we needed them. Asher hotwired both buses.

On the first bus was me, Dan, Max and the rat, Cody, Rick, Josh, Tyler, Asher, the old man and his wife Martha. On the second bus was Buddy, Amanda, Warren, Sara, and Isabella.

As we drove down the road, I looked back and saw the other bus stop in mid motion at the sign saying, *Welcome to Grady.* Their bus started going backwards.

Everyone else had noticed, too, and the old man yelled, "Don't stop! Keep going! If we stop, we might not make it. Keep going!"

We got to the sign welcoming us back to The Char and notice that it's snowing.

Dan asked, "Is it snowing? When we left it was sunny and

bright out here. No way it can be snowing in April!"

As we got closer, there was a hissing sound. *"Peakingas..."* We looked over to Max. The sound was coming from his lap.

Dan asked, "Is the rat saying my name?" just as there was a bright red light coming from the rat. Then *poof* the rat got bigger, there was a loud *pop* sound, and the rat turned into Paul.

Paul looked up at Max. Max said, "I never thought I would be so glad to see your face. I love you, man."

Quickly, Paul said, "I heard the men say that Max, Rick, and someone name Carl was immune. They were looking for them."

"Drive faster, Rick. Something is coming behind us!" Paul said.

Dan asked again, "Why is it snowing?"

Finally, we thought we were out of danger. We decided to go to the police and report this and get help for the others. Pulling up to the side of the building, Rick backed in, just in case we had to leave fast and make a great escape.

In the station, we saw the police running all over the place. "It's an emergency. They said aliens are coming to town. Save yourselves!" one of the officers yelled in our direction.

I looked at the others and we all ran back to the buses. That's when we saw the cloud coming our way.

"Rick, drive this thing!" I yelled. We screeched out onto the road and I added, "I don't know where we're going, but go faster!"

Rick said, "I am going as fast as this thing will go!"

Paul said, "What are we going to do? Where are we going to go?" Nowhere seemed safe.

We all looked back and saw the whole city in smoke. All of us were scared, and no one knew what to do. Drive away, sure... but where to go?

At the same time, Rick and Dan both concluded, "We're fucked."

 May

1996
Sami Ridge

A given cub can   cover
ground and   be.
One day   I opened my mouth,
found that   I could sing,
and that   others
lived   like me.

I know you.

You lay your biggest toe above the water's surface. If it's time, something will come.

But it won't. You know it, and you save the thought for future fun-scares; the heart spike, a great white shark, shooting up, a galaxy of cold water, taking you. The scenario too close to you to be fiction.

You're seated atop a wall. A cobblestone bridge and behind you is daylight, springtime, and an ever-reaching lawn of clover. You try to come here every day, if not to change the sky then to sort out the unreal world below it.

And before you is the ocean. Black, wanting, simple. It

wants *you*, but won't have its 'greatest' (children = egotists) addition for some time. Your face creases like smudged dough to grin and you smack your clammy little feet together, gleeful that dreams lack pain, and that there's an overhanging spiral of lavender weather touching your head just above.

There's no one here. Very few get to visit and because you're so young (four and a *haff*) this is exceedingly special. More special than Mom staying home to be with you or a fresh, blank coloring book. More honoring than Christmas or video rentals. It's equally special to the baby.

The baby.

Back with everyone else, it's baking in a tank. It's splotched, and orange, and held in a design with wires; and while that's troubling, coupled with the smell of scrubs and gloves, antiseptic and adult fear, you know he's now here on this plane, with you. You don't tell them that you've been assigned—you don't glower when they scold you for reaching forth and touching his boiled-egg of a tummy. Your smile is small because your date was kept. The baby—your *brother*—is your charge and you've been ready for such a milestone.

You look at your hands now. One holds imposed expectation, our full, and awful-sounding-name along the palm lines. Sometimes, when you clutch your Disney toys close their faults can shake and burn. Dreams can do many things but there's work to do before you can fix that hand. You stuff it in a pocket and appraise the other because the hand on this hemisphere holds the truth; the *second* answer you give when strangers ask what you're going to be when you grow up. It's a far cry from asking what you'd *like* to be, and obviously a test of a toddler's level of ambition. The truth isn't the easiest offering but you gently lay this hand, palm splayed, in your lap regardless. You're unwatched. Perfect.

But because you think this, the sky brings someone to you. You look and they sit flush at your side—much, much taller, and therefore somewhat disconnected. Their feet are white, their ankles have leg hair. Defined, in the older-way. They're—he's— scarcely playing *his* legs, and his battered hands say he's (you won't say *man*, and you can't say *boy*) not all well.

But the arch of his face wins you; the trajectory must've been softer, fuller, more sound at some point. This kind of angularity belongs to people who've lived a little longer—some portal stepped over long after where you are. You feel your own vibrancy run through nimble calves and unshaped fat.

Do you wear those training bras in places like this? It'd do no good to check. It doesn't matter here.

You can't be sure of his age. You haven't worked out 'teenager' from 'older woman' to 'that age that must be said carefully, if at all.' You can't give an age to him. And *sitting/sinking* into a shared focal point the question leaves with every new one that comes. He's here. That makes him somehow alike to you.

But his face holds another. You ignored it at first in a wonder but now begin your invasion; there's a girl's full mouth, her hair, her wet brow covering his like tracing paper. They fit so well that you wonder if their features belong, or if he holds her stubbornly in place.

And these are things you can't understand.

You acquiesce to this, as is your nature, and make short work of focusing a cone of guileless charm in his direction. Men and women are a foul combination, but little girls can spirit through convention's cracks.

Like water.

The ocean darkens just a touch.

"I fucked up," his still white lips said. "I fucked up with her pretty bad."

He laid the line down shakily. Some older people were like that, and some children, too. Sputtered language is a good sign that you're okay with being imperfect. Still, his voice was a bit weaker. It reverberated, like Dad's truck at a stop light. It tried, hard, but this one seemed to have long adopted this struggle as a feature. He made it his, like you owned your stammers.

If your ears could peel back like a dogs, they would…. But there was no pressure, no dare to this one's voice, and the statement floated on the air for you to add your piece. You look hard at him and smell the girl's cold hair. Her smiles were warm, she was always smiling, and posing, and being. She liked to gossip. She liked costumes. She liked hugging girls as pretty and small as she.

But her cold had a taste. A sick malnutrition only some found beautiful. There was bone, and shivers, and you feel a need to look again at the color of your own free hand. Still very young and red.

His statement hung still, waiting for you to reach up and catch but silence is your favorite response. It tests.

He looks at you. His eyes are so thin but you feel that they were once so big.

"What color are your eyes?" you ask coyly.

"Blue," he manages. "They were real blue. *Your* blue, actually. And…" He reaches behind his head to cup his nape, stopping, and curving it across his thin shoulder. "… straw-colored hair. Just like you." He bows his head and finally does swing a leg as if to be bashful. You decide that you like his pale pink hair. It scares you because Dad would hate it, but that sort of thing can't find purchase in this place. You scoot closer. You really like this boy-man.

"What do you like to do?"

"Has anybody ever told you that you should do interviews?" He grins with a sidelong glance. "You'd be a natural." And so you grin. Big, with a hum, like the cartoons. It makes the sky switch colors.

Suddenly he'd holding a stuffed bear. Suddenly he's wearing shades and he looks a little healthier with their given obscurity. He looks empowered almost, at the bridge of decision. He strokes the back of the bear's head with his thumb, reassuring some afterimage of memory.

And you're holding your Peter Rabbit—the toy you'd given to the baby. You knew it would fit perfectly through his tank's portal, that he'd get the message somehow. It would sit there all night, holding a piece of you while he slept.

Its fur takes on a golden tint in the sun on your side but you look and see that the boy-man's bear stays submerged in dull, tapeworm grey.

He looks to you and gives a sealed aperture of a smile. The impressions are weak and his lips seem to give into nothing, but you're not good at smiling either. Life is just too heavy. You both mean well but don't look it.

"I just got this back," he explains. "It was with her while she was holding on."

When women reconvene with death does the underside of their flying skin release all thoughts of childbirth? You wondered if maybe Mom died a little and that's why the baby's here. *Is that how things are born?*

"I put this in his tank," you say. "Right in the hole."

"Does he like it?"

"I think so."

Boy-man regards his bear, holding it at arm's length above the stirring sea. "Not all things are supposed to be liked," he murmurs.

When a woman dies she rejoins the cold as white as moon milk. You smelled the girl's hair a second time. Her scent was somehow stronger.

"What do you like to do?" you repeat, almost pleadingly. You could hear the water right below your soles. Was it angry?

When a man is born sometimes they shine too bright, like a sudden asphalt scrape. Older ones have to place them in tanks, you gather.

"Please?"

The truth brought cameras and printed words, speculation, an awful, unwelcome concept.

"I sang for money," he told you, becoming rigid with an adult reservation. "I did it a long time. And I did some dumb things, and if you ever have my choice someday, I'd like you to say no."

"Okay."

"You promise?"

"Mm-hm."

"Say no," he repeats. "You can do whatever you want but always head up. Go up, okay?"

"Mm-hm."

A man curves upward into everlasting death.
A couple falls forward into one another's breath.

And there's a baby; your precious maybe.

The water seizes the man's ankle and he's wearing your face.

You look at you, understanding forever in everyone who lives.

And you want to scream but you let it sink in your throat, in perfect tune to the submissive splash of your sinking stranger.

JUNE

Darling

Ellen Jordis Lewis

The 2019 Volkswagen Beetle flew along the freeway, which soon became the highway as Midge and Anthony entered Oregon. Windows down, volume up, their hair freaked with the riffs from the classic rock station. It was good but it was about to get better. They could now afford way more house but were aware that prices were rising thanks to transplants like themselves. They were climate refugees.

Midge turned the volume low. "Are we going to get bikes?"

Eyes on the road, Anthony pointed his chin at the open stretch in front of them. "Look at this," he marveled. "There's hardly any traffic. We can drive during normal people hours and not be stuck forever idling."

"So we won't make as much smog. Bonus." They both smiled.

"We're going to have to get coats."

"Sweaters."

"Scarves, even."

"Will we still have to conserve water?"

"Ha! They're practically drowning here." Anthony smiled

at the road.

"We'll have the best garden. It's so green."

Signs came up for Coos Bay.

"Research time." Midge fiddled with her phone. She read aloud from several tourist sites. They decided against Prehistoric Gardens with its homemade dinosaurs in favor of the coastal wildlife farther up. There were many tons of seals and sea lions as well as abundant tide pools crawling with little crabs. Then they hurried along to Florence where they planned to stay the night.

They found a brewpub decorated with glass floats, carved wooden seagulls, and knotted rope fishing nets. It was conveniently next door to a motel.

Their waitress introduced herself as Trish, told them the specials and asked if they were from out of town.

They nodded sincerely and placed their orders.

Trish wrote on her pad and asked, "You going to see the plants?"

"What plants?" Midge was thinking about their future garden.

"Um, Darlingtonia," she said, gesturing to Midge's phone.

Midge found them. "A bog of rare pitcher plants, located at Darlingtonia Wayside. Just a little bit north."

Anthony said, "Let's go tomorrow."

Trish nodded and backed off.

Midge muttered as she read from her phone. "It's the world's only park dedicated to the protection of a carnivorous plant. *Darlingtonia californica* are remarkable because their appendages resemble fangs. Insects get lured in and confused by countless glassy 'windows.' The plant has no digestive enzymes. Instead, symbiotic bacteria and protozoa break down the prey into easily absorbable nutrients."

Outside the brewpub, after they'd eaten and paid, Anthony took his girl's hand. "I'm tired."

Midge laughed. "More like buzzed. Anyway, you earned it, driving so far."

"That's so Oregon. Making an attraction out of plants."

"We'll wake up early."

In the morning, they hit some antique stores and discovered the glass floats like those in the brewpub were kind of expensive. The clerks at two of the stores asked, "Are you here for the plants?"

"Yeah," Anthony answered.

Midge said, "We can't wait!"

"Everyone's so nice here," remarked Anthony when they were out on the street.

"So much for Oregonians hating Californians."

At Darlingtonia Wayside, they parked in the designated area and passed a small picnic area, where one family sat unhappily. The parents were trying, unsuccessfully, to quiet their two crying kids with food.

A slightly elevated wooden boardwalk surrounded part of the bog. Affixed to the center of a protective railing was a laminated infographic which told Midge and Anthony the plant was also called a cobra lily and that, with climate change, most of the original insects in its diet had moved north so the plants were in the process of evolving to eat other things, such as detritus falling from the forest canopy.

The flora itself was short in stature with muted colors. Another couple loitered at the opposite end of the viewing area; all four of them attempted to find the specimens that had the most visible 'fang' appendages and transparent 'window' areas. There were several—quickly aborted—attempts at pointing out an insect crawling to its demise; the air was heavy and empty of life. Shoulders fell.

"Let's get a beer and go to the beach," Anthony sighed.

"I'm with you." Midge took his arm, her wedge-heeled espadrilles wobbling on the widely spaced boards. "But slow down. I'm trying not to break a leg."

They drove past art galleries selling blown-glass plants and shops that had t-shirts printed with plant graphics. They parked on the north side of town. In front of them was a church. No, a *cathedral.* Not one of those modern suburban constructions that look like the pioneer church of Cracker Barrel; this was a real stone cathedral, complete with Gothic arches and spires.

"Oh, wow."

"How come it's here?"

"Hey, we *are* in Florence," Anthony joked.

"I don't recall *Florence* having license-plate birdhouses and glass floats."

They climbed the steps.

Midge read the plaque: "Cathedral of Earth. Welcome, all."

The great bronze doors were open, reminding them both of the famous baptistery entrance they'd seen on vacation in Italy.

Their footsteps echoed as they walked to the altar where a kaleidoscope of blue and red shone down from the stained glass above. The atmosphere was humid.

"Pardon the moisture," a voice behind them entreated. "This is Oregon, after all." A man in a black frock had his hands out, gesturing to the walls; various leaks dripped into puddles on the marble floor.

"At least you don't have to worry about fires," Anthony joked. They explained why they'd left California.

The man nodded, sympathetic. "Evolve or die."

The couple looked at each other with confused expressions. Midge's face shone blue; Anthony's was red. The liquid on the floor dazzled with multiple colors all swirling together.

The minister placed a gentle hand on their lowered heads. A blessing. "It's all right," he whispered. "It's okay. You're helping the environment."

JULY

Lightshow
Maxwell DiMarco

Split up, boys! Those damn skin-walkers can't escape all of us!"

"Damn it…." Bastien hissed, his head darting up in synch with Alexandra's as the nicotine-forged voice barked from down the street. The mob was *still* after them; they couldn't stay put for much longer.

Bastien looked over at Alex, who nodded silently in understanding. Returning her nod, Bastien reached out and took her hand in his. Cautiously, the couple rose to their feet as one, peering out from behind the toppled dumpster.

At least their pursuers couldn't be missed: A conglomerate of gun-toting Brooklynites had just appeared at the opposite end of the street, the flickering flames of their makeshift torches piercing the darkness. His eyes narrowing, Bastien whispered, "No time to waste."

Keeping a firm grip on Alex's hand, he nearly tripped over himself as he took off at a sprint towards a narrow alley, but he refused to let either of them fall. One misstep could allow the mob to gain on them. And on this particular night, there was another factor the fleeing couple could never have anticipated.

There came a distant holler of victory. Moments later, a

burst of color lit up the city skyline. Bastien's heart raced as the brilliant explosion of fireworks instantly erased their cover of darkness.

"Shit—" The young man flinched, the vibrant sparks of red, white and blue sparkling against the windows of buildings far overhead. For a moment, Bastien thought it was over, and bullets were about to rip through their bodies. But when his head snapped back towards the mob, the group was still far away, totally unaware of the couple's whereabouts. Apparently, for all their patriotic bravado, the rioters were consistently incompetent at pinning down their targets.

As the sparks burned out in the air and the street descended back into shadow, Bastien stole another glance at Alexandra. She met his gaze, the fear in her eyes obvious. Bastien felt a pain in his chest at the sight but for her sake, he refused to let his own fear show. Reaching his other hand into the pocket of his hoodie and checking for his pistol, he spoke in a hushed tone as they reached the mouth of the alleyway, "No matter what happens to me... I *won't* let them get you, Alex. I *promise.*"

The couple darted away between the buildings, faraway gunshots and screams filling the air as they ran, then boisterous hollering and the screeching wail of fireworks igniting. Typically, the sight of fireworks on the Fourth of July was something to admire, a spectacular defiance of the night as America celebrated its independence. In Brooklyn, it was a sign of idiots not respecting the fireworks ban (which was arguably also independence, if not recklessly illegal). Tonight, these lightshows only served to display a simple message: Yet another group of rioters had finally slain their chosen prey.

Bastien and Alex had been incredibly lucky since the riots began. By all accounts, their chances of survival were slim. But he also knew that their pursuers couldn't keep this up forever. Adrenaline from a modern day witch hunt didn't transform fifteen overweight gun-nuts into tireless athletes, no matter how 'patriotic' they perceived themselves.

If Bastien had *any* lingering regrets about the two years playing for his high school football team, they had faded from his mind over the course of this night.

As they cleared the length of the alley and the buildings opened up around them, Bastien scanned the area: A four-way intersection, cars left abandoned from when the riots first broke out. The traffic lights blinked dully, their color-coded signals having lost all meaning and purpose. Even so, just out of habit, Bastien glanced to either side before pulling Alex out onto the crosswalk.

Halfway across, he felt a tug on his hand and stopped. Concerned, Bastien turned to Alex as she raised her hands and signed: *Should we find somewhere to hide here?*

As tempting as the suggestion was, Bastien shook his head. "Not just yet," he replied, restlessly looking back and forth down the derelict roads as he elaborated. "We need to put more distance between them and us before we settle for the night."

Alex, while clearly hesitant to remain in the open, nodded in response. She followed close behind Bastien as he led them the rest of the way across the road, more echoing gunshots ringing out from somewhere that the two couldn't place. Leaving the intersection behind, they passed by closed businesses, most of them heavily ransacked by the rioters. Eventually, they came to another alleyway and took a hard right back into the shadows.

"It sounded like the mob was going to search the area back there. And the intersection should spread them even thinner," Bastien considered aloud, his breath coming out in raspy bursts as he tried to maintain a quick pace. "Once we're past *this* alley, we should be able to start looking for a place to wait the night out. I know there's still some NYPD that aren't part of this 'revolution.' Maybe they'll get these mobs under control."

"I'd rather get *you* under control, pod-lover."

"Wha—" Bastien was cut off as he was shoved sideways into a brick wall, his face colliding with the stone. He let out a cry of pain, blood oozing from the gouges and scrapes. Bastien cringed and clenched his jaw against further sound.

A raspy voice breathed into his ear. "If you two thought this alley was your chance to get lucky... afraid to say, you're sorely mistaken."

"I *told* you, she's just *deaf!* That's it!" Bastien hissed; he tried making a move for his pistol, but his attacker pinned his arm to the wall. "She's not one of them! Get it through your goddamn skulls, you *maniacs!*"

A throaty laugh burst from Bastien's assailant. "Oh, *really?* Well, that's the first *I've* heard of this, but thanks for starting off on the right foot!"

An explosion of blue and white embers ignited overhead, briefly revealing the sneering, wrinkled face of a broad-shouldered man clad in full police attire. Bastien mentally cursed himself; this wasn't one of their prior pursuers, after all.

"L-look, *Officer,* we were...." Bastien saw Alexandra moving towards his attacker. Bastien desperately shook his head, trying to think of a way to rectify the situation. Unfortunately, his motion only warned the cop of Alex's approach.

Scraping Bastien's face further across the brick, the cop threw him sideways and turned on Alex, yanking his handgun from its holster.

"So, you're 'deaf,' huh?" the rogue officer challenged,

leveling his gun at Alex. "I'm sure you know that's pretty suspicious in this day and age." Alex raised her hands in response, eyes going wide as the cop's own eyes narrowed. He motioned with his gun to her hands. "You read lips, girl? Can you sign?"

Eyes torn between keeping her eyes on the gun or watching the officer's lips, Alexandra nodded rapidly, carefully lowering her hands so she could sign: *Yes. I do.*

The cop clicked his tongue in response to her movements, head tilting with a sneer. "Don't know what the hell that meant, but I'll take it as a yes." He hummed to himself. "So I assume you understand me." He used his handgun to punctuate his commands as he continued. "Make a sound for me. Deaf people can make noise. I need to check for *garbling.*"

"She doesn't need to do *shit!* She hasn't done speech therapy!" On the ground behind the officer, Bastien forced himself up on one knee. "Anything she can say won't be annunciated; it isn't going to prove—"

The cop shot Bastien in the foot. Bastien screamed.

"You have the right to remain silent, you pod-humping pipsqueak!" The officer snapped as Bastien crumpled in pain. With a scoff, the cop looked back towards Alex, who was watching Bastien in horror.

Please don't kill him! She signed desperately, her breath coming in weak, wordless bursts. But the cop's patience had gone.

"Listen, you little curly-haired whore." He snorted, pointing his firearm at Alex's head. "Nowadays, the preservation of *humanity* goes beyond race, disability, and any other trivial bullshit. I'm going to save us *all* some time and put you down now. If you're not a skin-walker? You'll have died for your country." Without any hesitation, the cop cocked his weapon.

Bastien shot first.

The cop screamed bloody murder as the bullet blew through his kneecap, his own gun firing as he tensed. Bastien leapt at the older man, tackling him to the ground. The impact knocked the cop's weapon aside, as Bastien rammed his pistol into the side of the cop's head.

Before Bastien could fire, the officer rolled to the side and grabbed Bastien by the shoulder, punching him twice in the face then shoving him away hard. Bastien grunted as he hit the ground but kept a grip on his pistol. Another burst of fireworks illuminated the cop as he scrambled across the ground to retrieve his lost handgun, swearing and grunting from his own wound and seemingly lifeless leg.

"No you don't!" Bastien shot twice but the bullets lounged in the other man's bulletproof vest. At least the force of the shots allowed Bastien enough time hoist himself up and throw himself at the cop again. They rolled across the filthy, glass-littered ground.

"Get the fuck off of me!" The officer hollered, trying to grab Bastien's weapon. "Concealment of a Claimed civilian husk is cause for—"

Bastien shoved his gun into the officer's mouth. "I'd sooner save a husk than let you disgrace that uniform a moment more." Bastien pulled the trigger, blowing out the back of the cop's head.

The officer fell limp, brains and blood a horrific mess beyond him. Bastien stared down at the dead man a moment then pushed himself to his feet. The bullet had gone through his foot but the pain of the wound and his battered face still made him light-headed... or was it just the adrenaline of the encounter?

"Fucking hell." Bastien ran a hand over the undamaged

part of his face. "At least my dad didn't live to see what became of the force." He checked his pistol then glared anew at the corpse. "That's the last of my bullets, too."

Another burst of color exploded far overhead; with the brief light it provided, Bastien was able to locate and retrieve the other gun, giving it a quick once-over. "Smith & Wesson M&P 5.7. More rounds than my Colt. Guess he did us a favor… but there's no way a fight like that went unnoticed." Bastien wiped down his empty pistol with his sleeve before tossing the useless firearm away, slipping the M&P 5.7 into his pocket as Alex came to his side. "If we can get a few more blocks between us and where the last mob split up, we should be good. We need to be fast but stay low to avoid anyone coming toward the gunfire and—" Bastien cut himself off as Alex placed a hand on his shoulder. "Alex? What—"

Another explosion overhead. Multi-colored embers burst through the air with a series of crackling bursts, allowing Bastien to see Alex's face. His breath caught in his throat, heart sinking as he realized what had happened.

Nothing needed to be said; Bastien didn't *want* Alex to acknowledge what he was seeing as a thick red line trailed down from what little was left of her left eye and temple. Their situation was undeniable. She signed three simple words:

He got me.

The distant sounds of gunfire were scarcer. Every so often, elaborate fireworks would ignite, lighting up the skyline to raucous applause, only to end just as abruptly. The rioters seemed to be wrapping up for the night, celebrating the lives they'd claimed.

Bastien only acknowledged this subconsciously as he and

Alex moved briskly down the street. He wasn't even processing the pain of his own wounds anymore. Alex wore Bastien's shirt tied around the left side of her face, the now-bloodied white fabric concealing her wound. Bastien's heart thundered in his chest. He cursed himself for losing their supplies to the mobs; their med kit was gone and the rogue cop had only empty clips on him. Apparently, he'd had quite a spree. If Bastien and Alex were caught now, it would mean the end of everything.

"We... just need to find someplace isolated... where no one will find us... just for the rest of the night," Bastien muttered, trying to reassure both Alex and himself. "Once the riots are over, I can go out, find you an eye patch, or bandages, or *something* proper to cover you! Just so long as no one sees—"

A hand on his shoulder made the panicking Bastien whirl around. It was just Alex. Though clearly anxious herself, she signed to him calmly: *I won't let you go out on your own.*

Bastien balked at her words. "I-it's not a question anymore, Alex. You're wounded! My foot... it's not as bad as I thought. The rioters are going after *anyone* and walking around with a bloody shirt on your face will definitely—"

A sharp whistle sliced through the night air. "Aay, you two! Over here!"

Bastien grit his teeth, tightening his hand on the handgun in his hoodie pocket as he slowly turned. "Look, man, we're not looking for—"

"—Trouble? Yeah, neither am I, pal."

The stranger waved at them from outside a store across the road. He was probably in his sixties, heavyset with a tawny blonde goatee streaked with gray. Clad in full patriotic attire—an Uncle Sam costume, and red, white and blue face paint—Bastien didn't recognize him... until the younger man spotted the nicked and dented Yankees baseball bat tied like a broadsword across the man's shoulders.

"Mr. Korhonen?" Bastien questioned cautiously, stepping forward a little.

The man let out a raspy but hearty smoker's laugh. "Bah-hah-hah! *Bastien?!* You scrawny little French bastard! You *really* can't call me Phillip after all this time?"

"R-right...." Bastien managed a weak smile, a faraway burst of fireworks making him jump. Briefly exchanging glances with Alex, he questioned: "So, you're not taking part in the riots?"

Phillip let out another big laugh until a hacking cough cut him off. "What? Just because I get a bit patriotic around the Fourth, don't lump me in with the rampaging Trumpublican nutcases! Nah, you little scamp, I'm clean! Now get over here and bring your girl. I've got a 'Things to Eat While the Country's Going to Shit' sale going on. All the jerky and chips are free!"

Bastien once more looked over at Alex, neither of them feeling very sure of themselves.

Are you certain he can be trusted? Alex signed, her uncovered eye making several darts in the direction of the shop owner.

Bastien sighed and murmured to Alex: "I'm not. But I've got no excuses and no better options."

"What are all those wacky hand motions? You lovebirds getting cold feet?" Phillip had to shout as more fireworks crackled and burst. "Because cold feet can be warmed up by coming inside where we *won't* be shot on sight. You feel me?"

"Uh... yeah, sure. Be right there, Mr. Ko—Phillip," Bastien relented. Taking Alex's hand, he whispered under his breath, "I won't let him hurt you."

Alex simply nodded.

Phillip swung open his shop's door and waved them over, the couple quickly crossing to his side of the street. Bastien stepped inside the store first, Alex remaining slightly behind him as Phillip shut and locked the door. Walking around the two as they examined the dark establishment, Phillip called into the surrounding aisles, "Alright, boys! We've got two more joining the family, and one of 'em is my boy Bastien. Get over here and make 'em feel welcome!"

"Damn it all," Bastien swore quietly as three more people came to join them by the store's entrance. Unfortunately, he recognized none of them.

"Pardon me, ma'am, are you alright?" The first of the three to address Bastien and Alex was a white man with short, brunette hair, wearing a light gray shirt and suspenders with jeans. "Hector Jones, D.O.," he introduced himself. Alex instinctively took a step backwards. "If you require—"

"Sh-she's fine!" Bastien blurted out, promptly stepping between Alex and the man. "She might have a hard time following. She's deaf and…." Bastien mentally wracked his brain, trying to find an excuse.

The doctor watched him skeptically, but the older man's attention shifted to Alex as she began to sign: *When the riots broke out, I cut my face scaling a fence.*

Bastien noticed the doctor was clearly reading her signs as Alex continued.

Bastien already treated the cut. The bleeding has stopped.

"Mm. I see…." Hector mused. Glancing at Bastien, the doctor eyed him for a moment in silence; Bastien silently prayed he wouldn't press him for further details.

Phillip took that moment to butt in. "Geez, Hector, lay off

the lady!" The salesman grunted, pushing Hector away from Alex with a beefy arm. "And wait your turn, I've still gotta get everyone else introduced to ole Bastien here."

"Um, I can just—" Bastien was cut off as Phillip threw an arm over his shoulders, dragging him over to one of the other two strangers.

"Time to meet Quarantine Crew 2.5." Phillip jabbed a finger towards a skinny young man around Phillip's age, his dark hair trimmed into a bob. "This twig of a dweeb is Diego... something. He's my hire of the month and my appliances guy; he had the misfortune of getting stuck here fixing the freezers when the first shots rang out this morning."

"Diego *Morales*," Diego offered. "Hey, Bastien." Diego stood with his arms crossed across his chest. He glanced aside. "I got a radio rigged up in the backroom if you need to call—"

"—And *this* lovely lady is Ms. Gianna DeSimone!" Phillip promptly cut Diego off, physically turning Bastien towards a statuesque woman in a button-up shirt and jeans, a shotgun strapped across her back. "No relation to DCE, the consulting engineers in NYC; I asked."

"It's also *Mrs.* DeSimone," Gianna interjected with a sigh, adjusting the ammo belt around her waist with evident irritation. "My husband and I are quite happy together, and—*again,* Korhonen—he is *very* much alive. I spoke with him over Diego's radio *literally* minutes ago."

"Well, shit can go down in times like these. You never know!" Phillip shrugged, only half-listening as he turned back to Bastien. "Found Gianna outside the store blasting some MAGA asshole in the face with his own double-barrel. I dragged him to the dumpster out back to keep his pals off our scent." Phillip smirked as he jabbed Bastien in the stomach. "She's not too bad a catch, eh? France, Italy—you're neighbors! Thought I would put in a good word for you, ya feel me?"

"Phillip, I...." As he addressed Phillip, Bastien looked up at Gianna with a sincerely apologetic look. "I don't really need relationship help. I'm doing fine on my own."

"Heh! Yeah, say that when you're my age, bud." Phillip chuckled. "But hey, message received; I'll let you handle things for now. Looks like you've scored a little missy since we last talked anyway." He lifted a thumb, jabbing it in Alex's direction. "I mean, she's no Donyale Luna, but who the hell is these days, right? And what you have going is cute, too. It's got that chocolate/vanilla swirl thing to it."

"Jesus *Christ*...." Diego pressed the palms of his hands into his eyes. Bastien assumed Phillips' well-meaning but grossly inappropriate comments were making Diego regret every life choice that had led him to being employed at Snacks 'n' Stuff.

Phillip, of course, didn't notice a thing, moving Bastien over to Hector. "And last but not least, my knee doctor: Hector. Now, he's the go-to guy for all the boo-boos 'round here."

"It's nice to meet you, Mr. Garnier." Hector's voice still held an undertone of suspicion as he offered his hand to Bastien. "I've heard *a lot* about you while working with Mr. Korhonen."

"It seems like most people have...." Bastien admitted wearily, shaking the doctor's hand then withdrawing just as quickly. He glanced at Alex then at Philip.

"So now you know my Merry Men," Phillip chimed in with a toothy smirk, clapping Bastien on the back. "It's high time *you* got introduced. Folks? This is Bastien Garnier—"

"*We know!*" The three spoke in a unanimous groan.

Phillip made a dismissive sound before looking at Alex. "And the beauty next to him is his latest—or quite possibly his *first*—squeeze, Miss... uh...?" Phillip stumbled over himself as Alex turned towards him and met his gaze. "Don't think I ever got your name, actually."

Alex turned to the rest of the group, a blast of blue and pink flashing outside as she signed matter-of-factly: *My name is Alexandra Davis. Bastien calls me Alex.*

Before Phillip could ask for interpretation, Hector clarified. "Her name is Alexandra Davis, Phillip. Bastien calls her Alex."

"*Alex!* Lemme tell ya, you're one lucky lady!" Phillip laughed, throwing his arms around Bastien and Alex before pulling them towards him in a half-hug. "This kid's folks were my holiday regulars! Any holiday at all but especially the Fourth, they'd come in and buy every seasonal decoration I had! They were real supporters of the little guy!" Phillip winked at Alex and jabbed a thumb toward Bastien. "Believe you me, Alex, if I were your age and had a clam in my pants? I'd get myself married to this one, too!"

Slapping the two on the back, Phillip pushed past his disgusted audience, crossing the eclectic corner store to the sole check-out counter. "Now you all know one another and we've got a long night of squatting ahead of us, so mingle among yourselves, folks! If you need me, I'll be in the office watching the televised shit show. Either that, or in the men's room making one of my own! Bah-hah-hah!" Squeezing his ample frame behind the counter, Phillip jerked open the door to his puny office and let it slap shut behind him.

There was an awkward moment of silence as if Phillip's over-sized personality needed recovery time, then Gianna pushed past Bastien and Alex to cautiously peer out at the streets beyond the glass. Turning back towards them so Alex could read her lips, Gianna asked in a harsh whisper, "Were you followed?"

"No," Bastien hastily replied. After a moment of consideration, he steadied his voice and clarified. "There *was* a group of rioters after us but we lost them an hour ago. We haven't seen any other groups since."

"Thank God Almighty." Gianna exhaled spitefully, moving away from the glass. "The last thing we need are *more* Republicans lugging bats around."

"As I don't own a bat, I'll assume I'm exempt from this generalization," Hector commented.

"You know who I'm referring to, Dr. Jones." Gianna motioned towards Phillip's office door. "How an unkempt, loose-lipped man like that has any friends outside of the bar scene is beyond me."

"Mr. Korhonen was my mother's best friend... and her ex," Bastien informed them, trying to shed light where he could. "My dad and I tolerated him for her sake, but he... well, Phillip tries his best with me now that they're gone."

"Oh." Gianna's voice softened as she realized his implications. "I'm sorry for their passing."

"Thank you, Mrs. DeSimone," Bastien acknowledged; Gianna nodded in approval of his courtesy. "I wasn't very close with my mother. My dad passed just last year—three years after I moved into my own place—so I can't *really* say I was unprepared." Bastien sighed, eyes quietly locking with Alex's own. "Unlike some of the others who are out there tonight...."

"How'd they pass? Your parents," Diego asked, his face illuminated by a faraway flash from outside. "It wasn't to the pods, was it? They weren't Claimed, were they?"

"Mr. Morales." Hector looked over at Diego, dismayed by the young man's blunt questions. "That's not appropriate."

Despite the stern reprimanding from the doctor, Bastien

answered Diego honestly. As he spoke, Alex took his hand. Her visible eye closed solemnly; maybe she didn't want to hear the story again.

"My mother passed two years back; she was older than my dad. Had a lot of health problems near the end. But my dad... he was an NYPD officer. He served on the force before I was born then rejoined when I was finishing high school. Anything to help pay for Mom's pain medication."

The store was quiet as Bastien remembered the sequence of events. Hector and Gianna watched him, knowing what would come next. But Diego was the one to break the silence: "So he was one of the first."

"Yeah...." Bastien finally admitted. Alex's hand tightened around his own, her eye open again and her face pained. "He was in Times Square when one of the first pods came down. It literally crushed a squad car. None of the officers on the scene were Claimed but... we didn't have any protocols then. And it didn't react well to aggression."

"Bystanders killed that first pod, right?" Diego questioned.

Bastien nodded in confirmation. "That was how we learned their 'brains' are in the center of their bodies instead of in their 'heads.'" Bastien elaborated: "It couldn't find a host to Claim in the commotion and apparently it didn't have time to release spores or to... 'scream.'" He shuddered a little. "If nothing else, I'm grateful my dad didn't suffer."

"I'm truly sorry, Bastien." Gianna sadly shook her head, bursts of color flaring in the sky outside. "These beings are disgusting creatures... remorseless, unholy parasites through and through."

"Potentially *mindless*," Hector added, placing his arms behind his back. "Protected dissection of the entities has shown no evidence of a physical encephalon. Some researchers are proposing that the pods are more akin to a mobile, extraterrestrial *flora* than fully-conscious fauna."

They've found no signs of mental activity? Alex signed curiously; Hector missed her initial signing but Gianna noticed the movement.

"Dr. Jones? Alexandra asked you a question," Gianna directed him. The man's intrigue piqued, he turned to the younger woman with his eyebrows raised.

"Yes, Ms. Davis?" Hector acknowledged. Alex repeated her question as Hector watched closely. He set his jaw. "Well, no. At least not in the studies I've read."

"Then those studies are wrong."

Hector then Alex turned to Diego, who was leaning against a heavy rack of magazines and mass-market paperbacks. "You have a knack for the inopportune, don't you, Mr. Morales?" Hector tiredly dead-panned.

"Yeah," Diego replied flatly. "But I'm right." He flipped through a magazine without really reading it. "My best friend's grandma found one of the smaller pods in her garden. Once she brought it indoors, it released its spores into the air and Claimed her. It used her body for months, even after quarantine started. All it took was one family get-together; just like that, Matt and his entire family tree were on the news. The CDC authorities, all suited up in their hazmat gear, dragging their Claimed corpses away… pod vines growing out of their eye sockets."

The store fell silent once again as Hector and Gianna watched Diego, wide-eyed. Alex clasped a hand to her mouth; Bastien placed a hand on her shoulder.

"You mean to say, *none* of them ever realized she'd been infected?" It was Gianna's turn to pry now. "But what about slurred speech or strained movements? Wouldn't it have been obvious?"

"Nope," Diego answered, a fiery crackle sounding as he glanced up from the magazine in his hands, staring Gianna dead in the eyes. "She already had problems walking and it faked a hoarse throat so nobody noticed a difference in her voice. Even before it got him, Matt even told me she mentioned some sort of medical care she was going to get. It explained away anything out of the ordinary."

Gianna raised a hand to press further but Diego wasn't done talking.

"It was able to write messages on paper. It was able to drink tea. It even remembered the full name of Matt's granddad. It knew its host had a family and was waiting for the right time... to Claim them all."

"Good Lord...." Gianna breathed out, her voice lost as she stared out at the distant lightshow.

Hector shook his head, tucking his hands in his pockets.

Alex began signing rapidly: *Have you heard any stories about the Claimed using sign language?*

"Alex—" Bastien began but Diego cut him off.

"Nope. That's the ironic part." Diego slapped the magazine shut. "The actual skin-walkers are more talkative—and more varied in their excuses—than anyone being targeted out there. I really don't get why they're going after deaf people at all."

At this, Gianna couldn't help but scoff. "Take a wild guess." She grunted, indicating the door just as distant gunfire rang out. "This is mob mentality at its finest: Idiots latching on to the 'easy' solution, resorting to blatant discrimination and violence instead of informing themselves."

"Just to play devil's advocate here," Hector mused. "Knowing they can manage long-term deception, don't be so fast to rule out suspicions." Gianna looked at him skeptically and he amended, "Not to the extent of the radicals in the streets. But clearly, further caution should be taken... or we wouldn't be where we are today. Any of us."

"Believe me, we've both been careful over the year. I couldn't live with myself if Alex was ever taken by them." Bastien swore, his grip tightening on Alex's hand... a bit too hard, causing her to make a quiet sound. "Shit. Sorry." Bastien quickly relinquished his hold and Alex signed: *It's fine.*

"Of course, Mr. Garnier..."

Bastien and Alex jumped; neither had noticed Hector had turned his attention to them.

"I'd only imagine you *both* would take intense care," Hector reaffirmed with a slow nod, eyes drifting like a spotlight over the young couple. "To say nothing of the threat Ms. Davis being Claimed could pose to others...."

Bastien felt a cold chill shoot down his back. "We've been together a year; I'd know if—"

"If she were Claimed, they'd know by now," Diego interjected once more, now flipping through another magazine. "If there weren't vines wriggling under her skin after getting cut on that fence? She's good."

"Diego..." Bastien began but Alex made a sound of worry and Bastien softened his face and tone. "Th-thank you, Diego. I... I think we've talked about this enough now." Bastien managed a sympathetic smile. "We've had one hell of a day and I'm sure talking about the loss of your friend is a lot for you, too. We should stay focused on the real threat."

"'Real threat?'" Gianna cut in, moving to stand beside

Diego. Both their faces displayed scrutiny. "Even with these idiotic rioters, that doesn't mean pods and Claimed hosts are irrelevant. The rioters are *another* threat, not a replacement."

Diego raised an eyebrow. "And talking about Matt isn't hard for me. Yeah, I miss him, but it made me more aware of how dangerous the aliens are. More people should know."

"Agreed, Mr. Morales, they should. I'm sure we *all* have the best of intentions," Hector inferred, stepping in to defuse the rising hostility. "And in fact, your comment did remind me: I should really give Ms. Davis's wounds a proper once-over."

Bastien's eyes went wide. "No!"

Everyone jumped. All eyes snapping towards him. Like a deer in the headlights, Bastien froze as he tried to reorganize his thoughts.

Hector took a slow step forward. "Is there a problem, Mr. Garnier?" Hector inquired, the cold validation lacing his words was not lost on Bastien.

"I'm... n-no, I'm just...."

Another wordless sound of distress from Alex and Bastien's hand reached out to hold her shoulder. He could feel her trembling.

"It's just... all respect... but are you qualified to examine a head wound? You're Phillip's *orthopedist*, right?"

"I'm the most qualified *here*. And I understand enough to comprehend the health risk that an improperly treated head wound presents," Hector responded matter-of-factly. He briefly looked to Diego, who was standing just behind him. "Diego, does Mr. Korhonen still keep a medical kit behind the counter?"

"On it," Diego confirmed, heading towards the counter muttering to himself, "Should have known when he went out of his way to show me it what I was signing up for...."

Hector returned his attention to Alex. "Ms. Davis?" he asked, hands rising up to sign in synch with his words. "For your own safety, I must request that you allow me to examine your wounds."

"Th-that's not... what if the bleeding starts again?" Bastien desperately argued, pulling back his hand and moving slightly forward so his shoulder overlapped with Alex's own.

Hector let out a quiet scoff. "That's *not* how this works, Mr. Garnier. You *did* pay attention during your biology class, correct?"

Bastien's eye twitched. Behind him, Alex's trembling increased; she looked on the verge of a total breakdown. Bastien could hear her starting to hyperventilate. His hand on the stolen M&P 5.7 tightened. No one was touching Alex.

"Doctor," Bastien stated plainly. "I'm not letting you uncover the wound. It's too dangerous."

"Dangerous... *how?*" Hector prodded, hands still deep in his pockets as Diego returned with a red first aid kit.

Diego raised the kit. "Do we still need this, Doc?"

"We'll see in a moment, Diego," Gianna answered in the doctor's place, adjusting the shotgun strapped to her back. "And if Mr. Korhonen has any anti-spore masks, I'd advise retrieving them now."

Bastien gritted his teeth. "Alex is *not* a pod."

"If she isn't, Mr. Garnier, you're currently making a very poor case for her," Hector rebuked.

Diego was already fishing facial masks out of the kit.

"If I may....." Hector took a slow step forward.

Bastien drew the 5.7. "Step. Back." His command was cold, arms shaking as he tried to steady his aim. "I don't want to do this."

Gianna leveled her shotgun at Bastien's chest. "Neither do I... so you'd do well to lower your gun."

"Not a fucking chance."

Hector let out a long, exasperated sigh. "Let me be frank with you, *Bastien:* I don't believe we're asking for your—"

"Eeeaaaaaaaarrrrrssesss!" Pushing past Bastien, a hoarse, garbled sound rose from Alex's throat. "Nnnnooowwwwrggggg!"

"A-Alex, *no!*" Bastien pleaded, clamping his arms over his head as the survivors whirled on the young woman. "I said I would pro—"

Alex's mouth dropped open, and she screamed.

The sound that emerged from her mouth was deafening; an unyielding, ear-piercing tone that no human could maintain. Diego, Hector and Gianna's sounds of pain were absorbed into the din of the otherworldly scream. Their hands clamped over their ears, they fell to the floor as the hellish shriek continued on and on.

Bastien keeled over as well, his arms only providing the slightest protection. He forced himself to keep hold of the gun as the others writhed in pain.

"Get... get to the radio—*now!*" Hector managed to sit up, shouting to everyone and no one. "I *knew* they were lying—"

Bastien shot him between the eyes. "Keep your suspicions to yourself next time!" He spat. Hector's blood spread between the floor tiles.

Alex's scream continued and the auditory pain was numbing Bastien's brain, threatening to throw him past the threshold of consciousness. The whole building felt like it was spinning; Bastien could feel his own blood trickling from his torn eardrums. The sweet silence of unconsciousness... but there was no time for that.

Phillip's office door opened with a slam.

"Well fuck me in my hairy asshole! Which one of yous was the skin-walker?" Phillip had his bat in his hands and plugs in his ears as he scanned the room, his bombastic voice audible even through the din rising from Alex's throat.

As if on cue, Alex was illuminated in a burst of red fireworks from outside and Phillip cursed under his breath. He smacked his bat into his palm as he rounded the counter. "For fuck's sake. Bastien's girl? Well... sorry kid, but I guess you're single again—"

Bastien shot Phillip in the calf.

The big man stumbled and went down, hitting the already-bloodied floor with a hard *whack*. Shocked, Phillip finally saw his shooter... as Bastien stared him down with burning fury.

"Bastien—"

Bastien shot Phillip in the head, finishing the job as gore splattered the counter.

Alex's scream declined in intensity. Her neck appeared to be sucked inwards and her voice became raspy. The pain in Bastien's head was replaced with a droning tone. But there were still two witnesses left.

Unsteady but determined, Gianna looked between the two of them, trying to ascertain which was the bigger threat—the monster with or without the loaded gun.

Bastien dove to the side as Gianna unloaded two shells at him. Apparently, the skin-walker's self-appointed guardian had been deemed the greater danger.

"You self-centered *lunatic!*" Gianna hollered, firing a second time as Bastien made a break for the shelter of a heavy shelving unit.

Staying low, Bastien raced the distance to the front aisle

as Gianna paused to reload. Skidding to a halt, he squatted behind a dense display rack packed with flags and tacky star balloons; he cringed as his weight on his leg reminded him of the bullet puncture in his foot. There was a burst of hot air as a third shot from Gianna destroyed a cheap revolving rack less than five feet away.

"You *knew* she was infected and you still brought her here?!" Gianna screamed as the store lit up with another flash from the shotgun and from the fireworks outside. "Are you *insane? Are you Claimed?!*"

"I *know* her!" Bastien snarled, lunging up behind the shelf and shooting three rapid shots towards Gianna, the bullets ricocheting off the neighboring shelves and dislodging several patriotically-patterned snack bags. Gianna took advantage of the reckless move and took another shot; Bastien dropped back down again, narrowly avoiding getting his head blown off his shoulders.

"You *know* her *corpse*—her Claimed and infested *husk!*" Gianna snapped, snatching two more shells from her belt and smacking each into their respective barrels. She dove aside as Bastien got off a quick shot, barring her teeth in a feral snarl as she heard him make a break for the opposite side of the store.

An extended period of distant hollers filled the air, rapid-fire bursts of crackling fireworks lit up the store in flickering lights. Inside, the two combatants stayed focused on one another, sprinting around the shelves and displays as they tried to land the only shot that mattered. All the while, Alex's scream was distorting into a horrible, mucus-laced choking, her hands rising to her throat and knees buckling as her windpipe slowly collapsed inwards.

Alex's voice came out in strangled bursts, a shaking arm reaching desperately to Bastien... but Gianna noticed it first. The sight pushed her over the edge.

"So help me God, you two can rot in Hell together!" Rage burning in her chest, Gianna leveled her shotgun and aimed straight at Alex's stomach—

Bastien's trigger finger was faster.

A second later, Gianna was falling back, her blood gushing from the hole blown in the side of her head. Her shotgun discharged into the ceiling and she hit the floor, dead. Bastien ran to Alex's side.

"I'm here, Alex. I'm here...." Bastien panted. Dropping to the floor, he took the young woman into his arms, feeling her weight fall against him.

A hoarse, sputtering sound came from Alex's throat. She wrapped her arms around Bastien's torso, weakly drawing him closer.

"Th-this wasn't your fault. I don't blame you! It was only a matter of time...." Bastien gently moved his hand up and down his lover's back, feeling her air circulation gradually return. "T-take all the time you need; I don't even know how you were able to sustain that for so long!"

"Thaaasssssshhh..." Alex began to relax in his arms, withdrawing from him, if ever so slightly. The eye left uncovered by Bastien's shirt looked back at him, bloodshot from oxygen deprivation.

"Let me help you." Bastien reached for the shirt but Alex flinched. "It's okay, we're alone. Diego ran. You can breathe easier without it, right?"

Alex looked conflicted but slowly nodded nonetheless.

Carefully, Bastien undid the knot on the improvised bandage. The fabric stuck briefly on the dried blood before Bastien removed it with a swift tug.

Alex hissed quietly as oxygen rushed over her damaged eyeball and Bastien watched as, from within her body, thin, green tendrils emerged. They moved and swayed in what seemed almost like curiosity, stretching out and up to Bastien's face as Alex struggled to speak.

"Baaaas... tien...." Her voice was slurred, stilted.

The tendrils made contact with his cheek and Bastien felt a trail of some kind of sap trickle down his face as they caressed him.

"It's... it's going to be okay." He smiled, undeterred by alien gestures that weren't so alien to him by now. "I'm not going anywhere."

"Neither of you will."

Bastien spun his head around, the movement tearing the tendrils and causing Alex to shriek in pain, falling backwards.

"Alex!" Bastien reached out to catch her, but the sound of a shotgun cocking demanded his attention. Bastien felt his face contort as he looked back at Diego. "You piece of shit!"

Bastien rose to his feet and raised the 5.7.

Click.

Nothing. He'd pulled the trigger but the 5.7's clip was empty.

And now here he was, standing in front of Diego... the last survivor of Phillip Korhonen's Merry Men, holding Gianna's loaded shotgun in one hand and a handheld radio in the other.

"Yes, sir, Officer. Bastien Garnier. He just tried to shoot me. He's a pod sympathizer," Diego confirmed over the radio, his eyes boring into Bastien's own. "He's out of bullets but the pod is still alive. Gianna and Hector and Phillip are all dead. Yeah. I'll see you soon." Clipping the radio to his belt, Diego held the shotgun with both hands. "I've got two shells. Why shouldn't I shoot both of you?"

"Diego." Bastien spoke through bared teeth. "You don't have to do this." He lowered the emptied gun to the floor. "Let us go and we won't harm you. No one else has to die tonight." Bastien straightened back up, raising his hands... but Diego motioned for him to lower them again.

"I think I misspoke. Sorry," Diego apologized, though his inflection was devoid of any semblance of sympathy. "I'm not giving you a chance to live. I just wanted to know how come the skin-walker is more important than all of us."

"Y-you...." Bastien forced himself not to lunge straight for the other man's neck. Taking a breath in and out, he relented. "She's... not like the others, Diego. Since we first met, I knew what she was, and why she was here. Because she told me herself: She just wants to *live*."

"She isn't even really deaf, is she?" Diego questioned, not acknowledging Bastien's words. "Did you teach her how to sign just so she wouldn't have to speak?"

"D-did you not hear me?" Bastien snapped, his panic-induced exasperation rising. "She's *different!* She asked for my help, so I helped her! Are you even listening to me?!"

"Sure," Diego replied flatly, eyes narrowing. "Are you listening to *yourself?*"

A hard pulse throbbed in Bastien's eye, his face ugly with anger. Diego's own eyes twitched at the sight but his face conveyed very little beyond that.

"One of us *will* be dead before authorities gets here. I just wanted as many answers as possible before then," Diego explained, priming the second barrel to fire. "Just doesn't make sense to me why you trust her, after everything I told you."

"Fine!" Bastien snarled. "Then here's your final

answer...."

As a crackling shower of red, white and blue sparks illuminated the store from outside, Bastien straightened and took a slow step forward. "Two years ago, Diego, I lost my father during first contact. This year, you lost your best friend and his entire family to a single alien. I have known Alex throughout the entirety of quarantine. And yet... even knowing that I had no additional relatives to lure in... *knowing* that I lived alone? She *never* hurt me."

Diego was silent as Bastien took another step forward; Diego took a step back, as if forgetting the loaded gun in his hands. "So that..." Diego hesitated, unsure what was happening. "That makes her better than us? You don't think she's playing you? Playing a long game?"

This time, Bastien was the one to ignore Diego's words. "Humans want each other *dead* all the time, for a million different reasons. But *she* doesn't. And if you want to kill her..." Bastien's final words came out in a roar: "*You'll have to kill me first!*"

Bastien threw himself at Diego, knocking the shotgun barrel down but it wasn't enough. Grappling at close range, the first shot tore Bastien's leg off at the knee. Screaming, Bastien went down, arterial blood spurting.

"Alex! *Run!*"

His vision blurring, Bastien could only watch in horror as Alex lay prone and Diego took aim at her stomach.

It happened all at once.

Alex's scream was fury and pain melded into one. Her body rose, riving violently as tentacles ripped their way out of her skin in a vertical line, from the top of her head all the way down her torso. And then... they lunged at Diego.

The man fired his last shot as he stumbled backwards in a

panic, Alex's head exploding in a mixture of blood and viscous green sap. But the tentacles weren't deterred and the target of their aggression had just squandered his final chance.

Extending across the store in seconds, the glistening tendrils grabbed Diego's limbs, locking him in place as the bloody mass that had once been Alex was hoisted upwards on still more connected coils. A hissing shriek rising from her severed windpipe, Alex's corpse slammed into Diego with a visceral impact, nearly knocking him to the ground in a splatter of blood and sap as *something* beneath her flesh pulsed and twitched. Diego tried to scream, to throw the pod off, but opening his mouth only allowed the deadly ringlets immediate access to his interior. In a flash of fireworks from the surrounding night, the pod ripped out his tongue and teeth, raged his throat and spread into his stomach and lungs, suffocating him from within.

Through it all, the pod continued, somehow, to shriek. The two corpses were locked in a writhing dance of the dead, a symphony conducted by the glistening, green tendrils of the pod. Was it feeding like a famished animal? Or avenging like an angel of justice? Barely holding onto consciousness, Bastien wasn't sure.

Finally, Diego's bleeding eyes rolled back in his head and the pod let out one final shriek... and ejected sharp tendrils out through his skin, exploding through his pores with a shower of tissue and blood.

From where he lay, Bastien watched as Diego's lifeless body hit the floor in several pieces, the remains of Alex still attached to the swarm of green. Overwhelmed by pain and quickly losing too much blood, Bastien made no attempt to react. He couldn't bring himself to move even as the tendrils crept across the floor. He didn't even react when parts of both corpses were lifted on those emerald threads, as if they were the grotesque body of a massive arachnid, the tendrils its legs.

Only when the mass had crawled to his side and set itself down beside him, did Bastien finally speak. "I... told you to run."

The pod's response was a slow, hissing ejection of air, Alex's severed torso shifting and swaying.

"And... now look at you." Tears welled in his eyes and Bastien lifted a hand, placing it on what remained of the human shell he had lived with and loved for the past year. "You... didn't have to do this. I didn't need you to avenge me. You *know* that you come first. It's... what we—"

A jolt of pain tore through his body. Bastien squeezed his eyes shut, tears seeping past his eyelids as he clutched his severed leg, feeling his blood run through his fingers.

One... two... three, then more tendrils extended from the mass of Alex's remaining flesh to Bastien's face. Bastien opened his eyes as they caressed him, their thin layer of sap mingling with the tears flowing freely now down his face.

"Wh-why... why didn't you release spores?" he pleaded, hardly able to keep looking at the tethered corpse that loomed over him. "It... you could have killed him instantly. Just planted a new pod and... transferred your consciousness to him... or to me... or...."

Another long ejection of air emanated from the pod. The highest tendrils began wriggling, then they shot down to the floor, snaking underneath Bastien. A scarce few wrapped around his arms and stomach, gently yet firmly, securing him in place, while the remainder joined together into a soft, sticky surface beneath him.

"Alex...." Bastien had a hunch what she was doing... and he knew if he let her go through with it, they would both perish. "Alex, just leave me here. The police will be here any moment.

They won't listen to us... not after what I did. Not after all this."

One of the tendrils holding his arm extended further, placing itself gently in the palm of his hand. Bastien choked back a sob, fingers closing on the tendril and holding it tenderly. "I-I'm not worth it. I told you I'd help you become one of us... and all I did was force you to harm others. I'm a horrible example of humanity and a sorry excuse for a partner."

The pod emitted a small burst of air at this but Bastien insisted, tightening his hold on the tendril in his hand. "If you leave now, you can find someone else... someone who can bring you the peace you wanted." Bastien stared up at the alien being at his side and forced himself to smile. "I love you, Alex. The best thing you can do for me now... *is to live.*"

Bastien expected the pod to make a sound at this... but no sound came. The tendrils still intertwining beneath him began to slow. And then, he felt the tendrils... retract.

Slowly, they rewound back towards their main body, all but the very lowest vines retreating into the fleshy remains... of Diego. The vines that remained out to support the creature began to rhythmically shift, rocking back and forth. They finally pushed Alex's torso upright and forward, causing her remains to fall, limp, across Bastien's lap... and causing Diego's torso to rise up, his arms, almost detached from his trunk, starting to move.

"Alex...?" Bastien asked, barely above a whisper, as the tendrils rotated Diego's body in place so it was directly facing him. The corpse's mouth opened with a ghastly hiss, a strangled version of Diego's voice speaking as his hands signed: *There is a way we can leave together. But I want your consent.*

"Alex...." Bastien hesitated, trying to sit up to see the signs more clearly but pain stopping him. "What are you...?"

I will not force you, Diego's corpse continued to sign. *But I*

cannot survive as I am now and I will not leave you. If you decline...
we will die together.

"A-Alex, I...." Bastien felt himself fading. How had he stayed so long?! "I told you... if it's between you or me? I'll choose you every time. And if—whatever this is—will let you live?" He nodded, partially to Alex, partially to himself, his vision blurring as his blood began to run thin. "Then do it. I don't care what happens to me. As long as you're safe."

There was a pause. Bastien was teetering on the edge of unconsciousness. Diego's corpse was perched but lifelessly, the tendrils keeping it upright quivering... and then its hands rose once more to sign: *Keep still. Open your mouth and do not shut it until I say so.*

New tendrils sprouted from Diego's sides and shoulders. Bastien's heart skipped a beat.

"Wh-what are you—"

A burst of fireworks went off as the pod threw itself on top of Bastien. The impact elicited a scream of pain just as swiftly interrupted by tendrils shooting into his mouth, nose, ears and eye sockets. Bastien was gagging, losing oxygen as he couldn't even scream in wordless agony. Then, at the climax, something he could only describe as his very brain being grasped.

In an instant, Alex corpse was gone. The store was gone. The *world* was gone! Bastien felt his entire reality turn inside out. He was falling, head over heels through a twisting, pulsating void, as the loudest din of voices he had ever heard bombarded him. He threw his hands up to shield himself from the almost tangible sound but the effort failed to even muffle the onslaught... for he had no hands, no ears, no body at all.

Yet still... he felt himself—*somewhere*—contorting, tearing, pops of adrenaline and raw, unfiltered agony raging through him. Bastien felt countless vines wrapping around him, pulling him in different directions, every tendril wanting to have him for itself, until finally he was ripped apart at the seams... yet his consciousness split with those limbs. Now he was in five places—seven places, twenty places!—he was *everywhere* and *nowhere* and the vines were sprouting from those limbs and reaching out to one another, pulling him back together across infinity.

"*Alex! Help me!*" Bastien screamed as vines erupted from his mouth, consuming the words before they escaped him. Tendrils came from his eye sockets and pushed out his eyeballs. Somehow, he watched through his own ejected eyes as his head broke into pieces, crumbling away to expose his brain, the tendrils sprouting from it like a million new brain stems. And every one of those stems had a voice. A voice that shrieked into ears Bastien no longer had, drowning out thoughts that were no longer his own.

He was thinking someone else's thoughts. He was feeling someone else's sensations. He was melting, he was freezing, he was dying, he was more alive than ever before, he wanted it to end, he wanted to leave, he wanted him to stay, they wanted him to stay, *she* wanted him to—

"*Someone! Please... kill me!*"

No, no, no! Not again! Please! Not him!

Alex's grip on her lover's mind weakened but it was too late. The absorption was complete; now, they were one.

Bastien was with her. Forever.

She had already harvested his final electron. There was no reason for her tendrils to remain holding onto Bastien's inactive brain. Yet there they remained, winding and twisting around his dead lobes as Alex listened to her lover scream for death in her mind.

What did I tell you?

She heard the voice of her original mate through the whispering, overlapping, weaving voices of her other partners.

It wasn't only the speed of the process that undoes them. Their race isn't equipped to be part of a greater whole.

I... Alex began but hesitated. She knew she should have listened to them. *I couldn't just leave him. I-I....*

We all loved him. We are as guilty as you are.

The voice of her last partner—the last pod she had merged with before departing for Earth—spoke then: *I know his suffering hurts us all. But his mental functions will die soon... just as they did with the original Alex Davis.*

They had meant to comfort her. But this reminder only caused Alex to give in to her despair. *I'm useless!* Her oxygen intake sputtered painfully as her mangled host body collapsed onto Bastien's equally lifeless corpse. *Why would I think hastening the process would save him? All I've done is hurt those who cared for me and yet I still think it right to take their names in succession?!*

Love makes us reckless, Alex. Another voice of her partners spoke up, their tone somber and nostalgic. *I still remember how eager my own totality was to join with yours. Such is in our nature.*

That's no excuse for following through with short-sighted plans. And to think... back home, they called me an ambassador. The corpse of Alexandra Davis shifted as Alex forcefully ejected the air within her primary bulb. Finally relinquishing her hold on Bastien's mind, she withdrew her tendrils, running them sadly over the man's colorless face. *I don't know if you can hear me anymore, Bastien... but I love you. I always will. Please... please know that I do....*

We all love you, Bastien Garnier.

As one, Alex and all her mates repeated this plea, slowly, again and again. They paid no mind to the small crowd that had appeared outside the store or to the distant voices beyond their totality that spoke from just out of sight. Only when the door was kicked in did their mantra conclude as an entire squad of officers swarmed into the store, their gun-mounted lights reflecting in the gallons of blood.

"NYPD! Everyone...." The armored officer's voice trailed off as her eyes fell on Alex still gently caressing Bastien's face.

"It's just sittin' there?" Another cop spoke up, the arm holding his weapon faltering slightly. "Bastard trying to get the sympathy vote?"

"I have no clue," a third officer replied, lowering the pistol in his hand. "I've never seen this in pod ambushes before... certainly not from a lone specimen."

"Men *and* pods have done things I'd never seen before tonight. Let's not take any chances," the armored officer responded matter-of-factly. Leveling her pistol at the stomach of Diego's corpse, she motioned for her fellow officers to follow her lead. "On my mark, we shoot the torsos together. That should also take care of any newly-laid spores."

"Locked and loaded," an officer replied with a smirk, leveling his gun at Bastien. "Stay right there, skin-walker."

"Ready!" another officer prompted, aiming his pistol at Alex's torso.

But the command never came. Instead, a low, resonating hum filled the night and swept into the dark corner store. The squad's focus faltered as they looked at each other then finally outside.

"My God… there are more of them after all!"

The humming rose to a crescendo and a scream rang out from outside the store. A crowd of rioters and citizens alike gathered at the door and around the surrounding squad cars, all of them looking up at the sky. One young man ran into the store shouting: "Officers! There's something's in the sky!"

Several officers cursed and most of them forgot about the debilitated pod collapsed among the human corpses. The squad leader was on her handheld: "Fresh pods inbound! I repeat: This is not a drill! Send all forces! Fresh pods—"

"Iiii… I ammmm sssrrrr…"

"Eh?" The officer staggered back as, gargling, Alex raised herself upright on her tendrils.

"What did you say..?" the leader demanded, her gun shaking in her hands.

With a great gust of air, emerald light washed over the city and filled the store, tinting the living, the dead, and the dying alike. People were screaming. Guns were firing. Another gust of air… brighter and deeper green lights… then another gust and another. Rapid bursts sounded in quick succession, like hot spring geysers, the series of expulsions swiftly approaching the storefront.

Throughout the city, the screaming and gunfire spread. Fireworks exploded in the sky, perhaps in fruitless attempts to strike whatever was overhead. The blasts showed no sign of impact and the myriad of lights were enveloped by the all-encompassing greens.

The few officers that remained inside looked at one another. One of them muttered, "What on God's green Earth…?" and another whispered, "Have mercy on our souls." They still pointed their guns at Alex; in a state of shock, what other action could they take?

The pod's tendrils raised Diego's limp arms and signed one final sentence to them:

I am sorry. They have arrived.

augUSt

Dear Diary
Bree Indigo

August 1, 1892

I finally mustered the courage to return home today. Emma came right back when we arrived in Fall River after our New Bedford "vacation" as Father and the Mrs. called it. I don't know for how much longer I can stand to live in this house with them.

The Mrs. served some old bland mutton, sat out on the stove for Heaven only knows how long. Emma and I refused to eat it—her more graciously than I—and no surprise, to me at least, both she and Father took ill shortly after. I told her it looked disgusting and she offered to ask Maggie to fry some poultry for me. Gold-digging hedge-creeper. She knows I still am plagued with nightmares of blood dripping down the walls of my sweet angels' coop. That horrid man will burn in Hell for the slaughter of those innocent souls.

I'm shaking just thinking of it. Father said the pigeons would draw youths into the barn but I know it was merely an excuse to take something from me. He doesn't dare permit mirth in his domain and those little birds were the bright spot in my day that he just could not stand. Thirty-two years on this earth and this is the life I am destined for?

I must stop writing. Father won't permit the purchase of any more candles this year and we must save them for the winter. All his wealth and we still have no electricity.

I grow weary of this frigid, frugal life.

August 2, 1892

There may still be some small joys in this life. The afternoon found Bridget and I alone and it is inexplicable the way her company makes me feel.

I never understood what Emma was speaking of, when she confessed of her nervousness around a certain man, the feeling of butterflies trapped in her chest, her heart fluttering and causing her to stumble over her words when he was near. I had never felt that with any of the schoolboys I grew up around, nor the few suitors who dared approach Father when I came of age.

But when I am with Bridget, it is like Easter Sunday when the morning sun finds the church window and you can feel the Holy Ghost shining down on us all as we sing our hymns of praise. Something fills my spirit when her eyes find my own, when her hand grazes mine—it is as I imagine flying would feel. She is my reprieve from this hostile home. My secret sanctuary.

That insipid cow Abby accused me of poisoning her and Father. I told her she looked hardly alive, so why would I bother? If anyone has poisoned them, it's Father's frugality and her insistence that the mutton was "perfectly fine". How dare she point her finger at me? It was her hand that stirred the mutton pot—figuratively.

Besides, half of Fall River has reason to poison Father, which he brought up *just last night*! Perhaps Emma and I should be happier that he has—mostly—refused to sell to us. He seems to double-cross everyone he deals with.

Speaking of, Mother's brother John arrives tomorrow. Hopefully, Father will not swindle him too badly. I find that despite myself, I am somewhat fond of him, if not only because he is a reminder of Mother.

God rest her soul.

August 3, 1892

The shrieks of pigeons filled my dreams, their panicked cries and frantic wings beating against the interior of my skull, a violent cacophony of fear and blood and pain. I watched them from above, helpless and frozen, until I broke free—but found that I was one of them. I saw flashes of Father's face coming at me, the axe swinging and finally finding its purchase, slicing through my neck. I watched my avian body fall from the loft as my screams fell silent and my vision began to fade.

I woke with a migraine this morning that refuses to abate, each pulse a painful reminder of the nightmare that preceded it. I resent him deeply. I dare say I think I hate the man. I find it more and more difficult to remember any redeeming quality or memory associated with him and soon I fear there will be no love left in my heart, for him or otherwise. He has blackened my soul with this hate.

Uncle John arrived late this morning, but Father has kept him busy all day. Selfish, loathsome man.

August 4, 1892

Something horrific has happened. Father is dead. Do I dare to write the word? *Murdered.* And his wife.

The day is a jumble and everything feels out of order. I will write down everything I remember. My head is still spinning from the morphine and so many queries from so many people. The police barraged me with question after question even as my head pounded like an axe had been lodged in my skull rather than Father's. There are flashes of faces—Dr. Bowen, Emma, and sweet Bridget's face filled with horror when she saw Father dead on the couch.

Father—his head split nearly in two, his lifeless body splayed on the couch where he slept this morning.

Abby, her limbs splayed at odd angles, the back of her head a thick, bloody mess, matted with hair, blood, and bone fragments.

My hands, sticky with blood, shaking in front of me.

The sweet satisfaction as the blade of the axe found its purchase, over and over again, each swing filled with retribution.

No. I must not allow these crimson thoughts to remain. I will purge them from my mind and burn them with the dress and these pages. They will burn, just as Father and Abby both burn in eternal hellfire.

And I will forget.

Lizzie Borden took an axe
And gave her mother forty whacks.
When she saw what she had done
She gave her father forty-one.

September

What Happened?
Diane M. McPhee

What happened to the little girl, Grandma?" I looked into the green eyes of my fourteen-year-old granddaughter and thought for a minute. I have told this story many times over the years, and no one has ever asked about the three-year-old girl. Somehow, she seems to have been lost inside my memory. Sadly, I don't even recall her name.

This story began forty years ago. I had just ended a short-lived marriage and moved from a small town in rural Massachusetts to Boston. Surprisingly, I had secured a job at a bank in the thriving downtown area of the city. At the time, I was so young and naïve that the idea of living in a city like Boston was daunting. Also intimidating was finding a place to live. Someone directed me to a street called St. Botolph just a block from Copley Square. I was told that young investors had purchased a row of townhouses and were remodeling them into apartments. It was just my luck that a first-floor studio was available. I also realized that this location would be walking distance to my job. Things were looking up.

My studio was one square room, a small bathroom, and a tiny kitchen unit with a half refrigerator. There was only enough floor space for a sofa bed, a small dresser, and a nightstand. I was the first tenant for the new owner, and I could still smell the paint on the freshly painted walls. The only thing that startled me were the bar jams on the windows and the police lock on the door. I couldn't imagine how anyone might break into the building since there were double entry doors as added protection. This offered me a false sense of security despite my growing anxiety due to being alone in an unfamiliar city.

The first week I moved in I met the owners of the six townhouses on the block. They were rich, educated, and interesting people my age. Proud of their accomplishments and seeing that I was in need of reassurance and comfort, they offered to squire me around the city. Weekends, and even some weeknights, we dined and danced, enjoying the freedom of being young and carefree. Even Sundays were occasionally spent calming our hangovers with Bloody Mary's at a popular restaurant that was steps away from the Boston Commons. After a few weeks, I began to feel comfortable and even delighted with my circumstances.

On my solitary walk home from work each day, I noticed some people in the neighborhood who were unusually strange. I began to admire the boldness of these guys who walked the streets in high heels and dressed in feminine clothing with elaborate makeup and wigs. When I asked my friends about them, I was told there was a house of prostitution at the end of our block. One of the most popular prostitutes was Maurice, a gorgeous Black guy. He stood out from the others because of his eccentric persona which was very entertaining. I began to look for him, which was easy because his outfits were beyond belief. He loved to wear feathered hats and tight satin dresses that accentuated his false voluptuous breasts. He was over six feet tall, and his makeup was bold and bright. His fake eyelashes were so long that I wondered how he could possibly see around them. Maurice was very friendly and loved to wave to people. As they gawked at him, he would smile his arresting, wide smile that invited one and all to come visit him anytime.

This is where the little girl comes into the story. At 2:00 in the early morning of a balmy September night, I was awakened by the scream of fire engines and police sirens racing down my street. Before I could even wake up enough to decide if this was a dream or not, my doorbell chimed. Fearing there might be danger, I cautiously opened my door, leaving the chain attached, to see what was happening. There stood a woman I had met only once who owned the building with her husband five doors down. She was wearing a blue cotton robe and screaming that her building was on fire. Beside her was her three-year-old daughter with tears running down her baby cheeks. This mother was begging me to take her daughter into my studio while she ran back to her house. I was unable to think of any reason why I wouldn't do this, and so I opened my door and let the timid little child into my single room. Her blond curls were knotted from sleep and framed her face angelically. We sat on my single bed, and I watched as her feet dangled back and forth in her little bunny slippers. I remember holding her hand and could only wonder at the complexity of her fear at such a young age.

I don't recall how long it was before her mother returned. I only remember that the sun had come up. There was a desperation in her voice as she reported that the damage to her building had been smoke fumes that had seeped through the walls from the adjoining building. Trying to hide the anxiety in her voice, she said that one building had been destroyed by the fire. The building that burned down was the home of the prostitutes. I found out later that Maurice had died in the fire. Apparently, he had a client who was not aware that "she" was a "he." During their interaction, the obvious became known and the customer went crazy. He was suspected of returning later and setting the building on fire. A wave of worry and fear hung over our block.

So now, the question my granddaughter asked me was what happened to the little girl? I only saw her a couple more times and she seemed very shy around me. At the time, I wished I knew what to say, but I didn't... at least not in a way that would make a difference. Eventually I heard that the little girl and her mother moved out of the city.

I told my granddaughter this story, not to worry or frighten her, but to reassure her that sometimes the most ordinary person can reach out to help just because they are living on the same street. I also hoped to empower her to have faith in her abilities and to direct them into a world worth caring for.

What I didn't tell her, was that after I had helped the mother and daughter, my days began to be plagued with events that seemed out of my control. My stereo, which wasn't really an expensive purchase, was stolen while I was at work one day. I couldn't understand how someone broke into my small unit without a key. How did they even get into the building which required a key that could not be easily duplicated. When I asked my friends if they had been burglarized, they all said no, but offered support to me. It was a comfort. But the following week, my phone bill arrived and listed several long-distance calls that I knew I did not make. When I called the phone company, they informed me that the calls had indeed been made on my phone, in my studio. We only had landlines in those years.

I became vigilant. I began watching over my shoulder to see if someone was following me. Every stranger became an object to observe or dodge on the street. I double checked the lock on my door whenever I left my building and made certain I stowed my key deep in my purse. When I met my friends for a night on the town, I insisted someone walk me home and wait until I was safely inside. Sometimes it seemed an inhuman effort to act normal and take part in things that appeared so easy for others. The loneliness of it made me even more anxious.

After a few weeks, as the September weather remained warm and my walk home seemed less worrisome, I began to relax and feel a little more confident. And then one night, it happened.

I was awakened from a deep sleep by the sound of scratching on my window. At first it sounded like a branch hitting the building, so I wasn't too concerned. Even though I had left the window open about eight inches, I knew the security bar was in place and would jam if someone ever wanted to get in. Annoyed by the continuing sound, I finally sat up in my bed and was shocked to see that someone was actually trying to get through the window. He had his arm reaching through the small opening and was attempting to release the security bar. I was paralyzed with fear, yet unable to scream. There was nothing in my young adulthood that prepared me for something so terrorizing. I remember trying not to breathe as I watched this person struggling to enter my room, a place I felt safe. Finally, as if someone pushed me into action, I reached for my phone, which was always beside the bed, and called 911.

"Someone's coming through my window," I whispered.

"What's your address?"

When I quietly said where I lived, she only asked one thing, "Front or back?"

"Front."

I remember rolling to the floor, still in shock, as I heard

sirens in the distance come closer and closer to my street. Whoever was pushing through my window, must have heard the sirens too because he quickly released his arm from the window. He was gone before the police arrived.

Bravery is used to describe a person based on their actions. Was I brave that night? I've often thought about this over the years. Why didn't I run out of my studio and call for help? Why didn't I scream when I recognized the danger? What surprised me that horrible night was my ability to pick up the phone and call 911 without having to think about it.

Fear is a terrible companion because it is such an unpleasant emotion. We all want to think we will survive a trauma or, at the least, react with common sense. It would be interesting to suggest that courage is an antidote to fear. But let me tell you, when the time comes, I hope you will have the willingness and ability to exercise all the courage possible when facing fear.

OCTObeR

But I Will Not
Pauline Ugalde

12:55 PM

My parents' sudden request that I take the rest of the week off, from Wednesday onward, doesn't seem real, even as they say goodbye.

My assumption that they changed their minds lingers, even as dad shuts my door, locks up, and pulls out of the garage. After five minutes, the house remains silent.

The celebration starts small: Waking up around eleven-thirty, skipping exercise, playing videogames and loud music, and eating lunch half past noon, accompanied by moderately fizzy fruity sparkling water. As I portion out my food, my iPhone on the counter, volume cranked up to high, plays a long YouTube video. I make jokes aloud to an empty room, that usually stay in my head. "No. Holy shit Shayne! You're too humble! Your friends wouldn't complement your brains and your gloots if they didn't mean it! In all fairness though, that's why we love you... ."

Either that, or start watching Pokémon Master Journeys again so I can talk about it with the cousins the next time we hang out?

I grab one—two—three—slabs of chocolate, and prepare

some liquor with ice, setting both on the floor far away enough I won't step on them or knock them over. Hauling my Magic cards box out of storage, I set it down, laughing aloud, not for the first time, about how I could bludgeon someone to death with it... if I was strong enough to do it, and if it had a second handle.

Not a moment after finding the right anime episode, and skipping the intro, does the speaker in the living room, separated from my bedroom by only a wall, activate. The doorbell rings.

I freeze for a moment, before remembering what my parents said. Pausing the Pokémon Master Journeys episode, I grab my phone off my desk and check for a text from my cousin.

Is it Amazon again? Is it mom's shoes?

Holy crap—are those my figurines?

I dictate a text to my cousin with my phone's voice-to-text feature: "Where are you?"

Phone in my lap now, I switch to my email tab while I wait. On reflex, even as I refresh the page, I make as little noise as possible. Just in case that isn't my cousin, I don't want anyone to know I'm home. I press T, to navigate to the table containing my email inbox, followed by U, to scroll automatically down to the next unvisited link, the first unread—

The doorbell rings again.

Again, I freeze, waiting several seconds before proceeding, straining to hear familiar voices outside. Jerkily, I press U, my screen reader announcing the subject line of the email. I press U again, continuing—

The doorbell rings again.

Lifting my hands from the USB keyboard on my lap, avoiding touching it like it's lava, I tilt my head to one side, in the direction of the—

The doorbell rings a fourth time.

1:00 PM

Who would question me, in broad daylight? Who would think I meant to break in, if I didn't have everything I'd need?

No mask to hide my face completely? No sunglasses? No hoodie?

No blunt object for shattering a window? No bag of holding to stash my spoils? No getaway car?

No firearm to dispatch the homeowners— No. Even better: No knife, sharpened, oiled, and slim, to kill someone silently?

No. I don't need those things.

Everyone who isn't cold enough to wear jeans, a jean jacket, and long socks this afternoon, is just lying to themselves.

"Fuck this. I'll do it."

No one could stop me, even if they tried. If they called the cops, what would they say? Besides, even if someone did call the cops, I know how to kill Karens.

I turn the corner and take another lap around the block. On the outside, I'm calm and walk with measured strides.

On the inside, I'm on the verge of strangling the nearest pedestrian, while screaming until my lungs give out.

I halt at the edge of a crosswalk before crossing the street in a daze. My eyes physically focus forward, but once again, I root my actual attention elsewhere. Pulling my phone from my pocket, I concentrate on the screen, ensuring I hold it in my head: A photograph from the chest up, taken with a shaky hand.

I quicken my pace.

Can anyone see this?

If someone does, will they suspect me?

If someone did, how much should I care?

I nod once firmly. My lips curl into a small, self-assured smile. Raising one hand, I motion forward, my index finger straight.

As vividly as if she's right in front of me, I see her, freezing as she reaches for something—

Her phone.

She listens to her phone for a moment, and her lips move, before she goes silent. A keyboard lies on her lap, and a closed laptop hums on her desk. I can't see what she's reading, but that doesn't matter.

What matters, is that I know that she's typing.

I nudge my index finger forward a second time, then a third.

Both times, she freezes.

Just as I thought, she tilts her head toward her front door, straining to hear someone outside. As she goes still, I ring the doorbell a fourth time.

I can see only her face clearly, but it's enough. She's putting her keyboard down as quickly and silently as she can. She's pulling her window and curtains closed. She's walking out of her room, body already angled toward her kitchen doors, poised to confirm they're locked.

Unapologetically, I laugh, long, high, and clear. "Heh! Perfect."

1:05 PM

"Okay. Good. They're locked," I confirm aloud. "Obviously, I have to deal with the window, now, but the blinds are so far away... ."

I can't find a stool, so I have no choice but to strain on my tiptoes. Just as I thought, I can't figure out how to close the blinds with solely touch. I can barely do it on my own when my parents are home, so of course I can't do it under duress.

My bedroom's and house's windows and curtains now closed, and newly-filled water bottles in hand, I breathe easier, for now. Before I give in to my urge to enact my whole plan, I remove all doubt. Fumbling for my phone, I dictate a message: "Are you or Dad expecting a package?"

My phone's voiceover reads the message as I tap it: "I ordered shoes. Don't open the door, okay?"

I text back, in an exasperated tone: "I know, I won't. When did you say auntie was coming over to check on me?"

It only takes a second for the reply to appear: "Around seven. She'll text you."

"Okay, good," I reassured myself. "So I can do this. But I have to tell someone so if something happens... ."

Monadofy

Today at 1:08 PM

Someone kept spamming the doorbell at my house.

Mode

Today at 1:08 PM

Why?

Monadofy

Today at 1:08 Pm

My cousin was supposed to come during lunch but he never did.

Today at1:08 PM

Mom's expecting a package but the mail people don't spam the doorbell.

Today at 1:08 PM

(insert joke about Mormons or salesmen here)

Mode

Today at 1:08 PM

> Did they leave?

Monadofy

Today at 1:08 PM

> Don't wanna check...

Mode

Today at 1:08 PM

> When are your parents gonna get home?

Monadofy

Today at 1:09 PM

> (shrug) Hella? Sunday afternoon?

Today at 1:09 PM

> Checked the doors and I think the curtains are closed...?
> And dad has security cameras so...

Mode

Today at 1:09 PM

> If you say so. I'll be here if you wanna talk. Be careful man.

Monadofy

Today at 1:09 PM

> Of course I will.

Today at 1:10 PM

> (cue joke about the horror movie rules)

"Thank fuck he's not busy—because I don't know what I'd do if he was... ."

As the familiar, muted thud of the enemy's attack breaks my defenses, I switch to the tab containing the cards in my hand, already finished internally sequencing my turn. I switch to the text entry prompt and type the index number of the first card I want to play, but before I can send the command, my phone pings again.

I freeze.

The sound is very similar to Entropy's message receipt sound, because the first note is the same, but that's where the similarities end. The second note is two semitones lower than Entropy's, and the whole notification sounds one octave higher overall. It also sounds more chiptune, like a jingle from an eight-bit video game.

The dev team just released patch notes for the latest update yesterday. They didn't say anything about customizing sounds. Not even for the paid version.

Fully intent on my phone now, I open the Entropy app itself, instead of merely reading the notifications from my lock screen.

Today at 1:11 PM

Shame you didn't visit the event on the last floor.

Today at 1:11 PM

You liked it.

Today at 1:11 PM

Taking all that damage hurt but it was worth it.

Today at 1:11 PM

Sacrifices must be made, and all that.

Just as I put my phone down and lock it, more messages arrive. The notification sound is still different from normal.

Today at 1:12 PM

We both know you're not actually tipping the scales.

Today at 1:12 PM

But I can fix that.

Mashing my fingers against my phone, I close Entropy and open my family's group chat, about to explain that I've been hacked. Just as I type the first letter, more Entropy posts appear, seemingly all at once.

Today at 1:12 PM

Just come out and take it.

Today at 1:12 PM

No one will see.

Today at 1:12 PM

But since you're still in your room?

Today at 1:12 PM

You already knew that.

1:17 PM

Every word is true, of course. Lying would be self-sabotage. If she realized I lied, she'd never believe what I said.

If she refused to believe what I said, I'd never see anything new.

Nothing would be fun anymore.

Physically, I'm at the park for the second time today. Simultaneously, I hear the rustling of the dry lawn in the wind, the gravel crunching under my shoes, and feel my fingers grazing the front door.

Each is a possibility, playing out in the immediate past, present, and or future.

Externally, I'm sitting on a seemingly random bench, leaning back, ankles crossed, taking in the surroundings.

Internally, I submerge in the probability function. I ride the wave.

People only experience a subset of possible outcomes.

Sometimes, that person reaches the same conclusion by taking different actions. Other versions of them decohere, and never intersect again.

I'm not like them.

My errors and their foreshadowing flash before my closed eyelids. Her unanswered, anxious shouts out her front door, her anger toward my intrusion, her simultaneous knife brandishing and phone clenching?

All and none of them happen.

This notification sound is exactly what you think it is. You're right, Monadofy.

These words flood me with a new, convergent outcome: One where my desires are my hands. Every external security camera, now piled together, sinks into the nearest trash can. False footage of the undisturbed house overwrites their feeds.

You really think I'd settle with doing this from afar?

With anyone else?

Somehow, I remain silent, as I transmit my laugh faithfully through an attached audio file.

1:27 PM

I have to do this, but I can't tell them. They'll think I'm crazy. They'll never let me stay home alone ever again.

"Or worse?" I admit aloud. "They'll come home."

In case I don't get another chance.

Monadofy

Today at 1:27 PM

Someone hacked my laptop and phone.

Today at 1:27 PM

They know I'm talking to you.

Today at 1:27 PM

And the games I'm playing.

Today at 1:27 PM

And the mods I have installed.

Today at 1:27 PM

Even the Inscryption one.

Today at 1:28 PM

But they're letting me talk to you.

Mode

Today at 1:28 PM

Did you tell your parents?

Monadofy

Today at 1:28 PM

I was gonna but

Today at 1:29 PM

The hacker said they'd have no way of knowing.

Today at 1:29 PM

They hacked my phone too.

Mode

Today at 1:29 PM

How do you know he knows?

Monadofy

Today at 1:30 PM

I heard his voice when I read his posts.

Today at 1:30 PM

He overrided my voiceover on my phone.

Today at 1:30 PM

But he doesn't have a username.

Today at 1:30 PM

> Every time he messaged me except the first time he replaces the notification sound with the Undertale Undernet status sound.

Today at 1:31 PM

> OH FUCK

Mode

Today at 1:31 PM

> WHAT

Monadofy

Today at 1:31 PM

> He did the doorbell thing.

Today at 1:31 PM

> He

Today at 1:31 PM

> He knows my keystrokes

Today at 1:31 PM

> And also he can—could—see me.

Today at 1:32 PM

> He doorbelled when I was texting my parents.

Mode

Today at 1:32 PM

> At least your devices are okay???

Monadofy

Today at 1:32 PM

> I think? Screen readers act weird if my computer has a virus.

Today 1:32 PM

> Doing a quick scan now.

Mode

Today at 1:33 PM

How long will it take?

Monadofy

Today at 1:33 PM

(shrug) Haven't done this in forever.

Mode

Today at 1:33 PM

Keep me posted.

Today at 1:33 PM

My schedule's clear now.

Today at 1:33 PM

I'll be here.

Monadofy

Today at 1:33 PM

Thanks dude.

Today at 1:33 PM

Guess I was wrong—it's like 90 seconds tops.

Today at 1:34 PM

I don't think you can do antivirus scans on iPhone but I'll check.

Mode

Today at 1:34 PM

But he'll see.

Monadofy

Today at 1:35 PM

Either he can't see it and the scan's fine or

Today at 1:35 PM

If he stops me I'll know.

Today at 1:36 PM

Quick scan's done.

Today at 1:36 Pm

>Nothing.

Mode

Today at 1:36 PM

>How long will a full one take?

Monadofy

Today at 1:36 Pm

>Hella…?

Today at 1:36 Pm

>But I have to.

Mode

Today at 1:36 PM

>Okay.

Today at 1:36 Pm

>I'll grab food. I have my phone with me.

Monadofy

Today at 1:37 PM

>Good.

"He already knows I'm talking to Mode so I can't endanger Mode by telling him."

The second-to-last item I grab from my room is my deactivated laptop. I only reboot it after setting it on the floor, close to my safe room's outlet, occupied with my chargers, next to the closest cordless landline phone I could find.

The whetstone isn't quite where I thought Dad kept it. I'm definitely performing the wrong motions. Still, both edges pass the paper test, and my dagger's structural integrity seems intact.

At last, I push Dad's recliner against his closed office door and enter the safe room, closing the door separating it from Dad's office, not even a wingspan apart from the room's opposite wall. I start the full antivirus scan, and boot Slay the Spire in the other tab.

Monadofy

Today at 1:42 Pm

Still there?

Mode

Today at 1:42 PM

Yeah.

Monadofy

Today at 1:42 Pm

Full scan's started.

Today at 1:42 PM

Let's do this.

Today at 1:42 PM

You won't kill me, bitch. Not today.

2:30 PM

There isn't a problem, and you know it.

During the COVID-19 pandemic, New York city residents could get cocktails delivered to them.

How is three coffees in one order weird to you? It's not the caffeine that focuses my senses and grounds me in the exact realities I want to see.

No. It's the cold.

After all, my heart is pounding in excitement, many times over.

The ride back to her house is as smooth as the one I took to lunch. The driver and passenger only see and hear what I want them to see and hear: No one at all.

Masks cutting off everyone's peripheral vision doesn't

hurt, either.

It takes all my willpower to resist the urge to grab the driver by the collar. In multiple, divergent instances, those feelings lash out at their car: Blown stereo speakers, shattered windows, or doors slamming open or shut.

In this timeline, though, I only vent after I've picked a new spot in the park.

"Why?"

My screams tear free from my mouth and mind. "Why can't I see you? You don't know! You shouldn't know! You shouldn't be able to stop me!"

Even while I squeeze my eyes shut, hands rigid in front of me, Monadofy's face is as detailed as if she was here.

Mouth taught with frustration, first one hand, then the other, strikes her.

The motion, amplified by the likeminded versions of myself, shatters one cheekbone, then the other. It inflicts one black eye, then another.

Metal shrapnel, unable to withstand my strength, shred skin, flesh, and muscle. Shards of broken glass pierce her skull.

When I'm done, Monadofy from the shoulders up resembles a destroyed phone screen made flesh...

I go still.

I open my eyes. I glance around, searching for frightened bystanders or frantic hands, dialing 911. I see none.

To everyone around me, it's as if I never moved.

No one noticed my outburst.

You can't get angry at her for doing this. She's the reason you're here. You can't blow up the safe to get the payload. You didn't lose control, like last time.

Even now, no one noticed you. This confirms that you've

gotten stronger.

In one smooth motion, with one hand, I summon the remains of the maimed phone from the ground, so they float above my upturned palm. Then, I direct a shard of glass to make a shallow cut across my opposite forearm, the latest in a long line of them. I trickle the blood onto the remains of the phone.

The pain is temporary.

The phone crumbles.

I pull the first of many burner phones from my pocket, without moving or looking away.

You've come too far to stop. To see the future where you succeed, you have to start.

I proceed at a jog, bystanders' eyes looking through me. On the sidewalk, I break into a run.

When someone got in my way? I shattered them.

The instant before I vault a parked car, as naturally as if I've done it a thousand times, I take in a deep breath and let out another long, high, clear laugh.

"For me, time is meaningless. Space is fluid. Things change. But I will not."

3:15 PM

Twenty minutes after the full, uneventful antivirus scan ends, my vigilance begins to wane. I even put both earphones in and tune out most random noises from outside. I still don't want to return to my room, let alone undo my security precautions, though. Even as my desire to sleep looms, I still have the forethought to place my phone and dagger next to me on the floor. I was wrong, but not about this room being a better place to sleep than I thought. I was wrong about my assumption that I would lack the want to sleep.

Within thirty minutes of the scan, my heart isn't pounding out of my chest anymore. At the fifty minute mark, the adrenalin has worn off almost completely. Sometime after three o'clock, the crash soon follows.

Face-down, with a pair of pillow refugees to either side of me, the paradoxical absurdity and logic of my predicament hits me. I spent months locked down in my own home for the common good, during the most severe waves of the COVID-19 pandemic. As frightened as I felt back then, the surrealness of the situation, comparisons to a zombie apocalypse and all, blunted most of that fear, or perhaps, concealed it so I could get by from day to day. During this time, only egregious losses of life, and acts of stupidity and malice, broke through my emotional safeguards. All of my cousins' jokes, and plans that were more detailed than we cared to admit to anyone else, about what we would do if the zombie apocalypse came true, came to pass, in the worst possible way.

Contrary to our plans, the act of us meeting constituted the danger.

This cyberattack and stalking combines my worst unrealized fears, with one I acquired through real life: Mass shootings, threatened and real. My only solace, and the only reason I can even fall asleep at all, is my familiarity with mass shooters' psychology. They go after vulnerable people and places. They don't kick down doors or break down barricades, because it's too difficult.

He doesn't see me as subhuman or unworthy to live. He knows me as well as my closest friends, and even knows me well enough to predict my gaming habits. If he knows my Slay the Spire mods, then he knows I use a screen reader, so he knows I'm blind. The only way he could say my parents wouldn't know I let him in, was if he knew where we installed our cameras. We both know I couldn't even tell him where they were under torture.

Whoever this person is, camped outside my home, doesn't want to kill scores of people. He just wants to kill me, but somehow, he can't. That's why he's taunting me instead.

Trailing my fingers along the floor, I slide my phone a couple inches closer, and my dagger closer still. "Either I'm tired as fuck and you break in so I die anyway, or I'm fresh and you break in but I shank you so you can't run away." I mutter to myself into my pillow. "I've been scared of getting shot in the head too many times in my life. But that was at school. I wasn't safe there. But I know how safe I am here.

"I can't run. But I'm not hiding. I'm fighting. You can't taunt me if you don't know what I'm doing."

My posture finally relaxed, I mumble one last challenge, before turning the volume on my phone nearly all the way down. "We both know, if you get in? You'll be dead where you stand."

3:40 PM

I only realize I've reached her house when I open my eyes, and nearly slam my face into the gate. "Shit!"

Peeling off and tossing my jacket aside, I confirm that the street's deserted. "I hung around there too long." Even as I speak, the sting of a face palm rises on my forehead. "Why did I do that? Why did I wait?"

Heat, rising from my chest: A recursive flush of anger. "She was right there. She was right there!"

Even as I scream into the ether, I clamp my hands over my ears, but it's not enough. The adrenaline crash, physical overexertion, sensory overload, and dehydration, compound.

Words hissed through clenched teeth, fueled by ragged

breaths: "I have to wait. But I don't want to. But if I don't? She'll kill me."

My inert body lies across the path face-up and blocks the gate. A hive mind human log. Even asleep, my visualized intent still coats me, and the ground I tread on Monadofy's property. My footprints remain smoothed over, and the vegetation undisturbed.

Everything is exactly the same, as if I did not exist.

The disturbance begins at the very edge of my peripheral vision: Physical, sensorial, and cognitive.

The mirage slowly grows and multiplies. Curious, I crack my eyes open, but go still.

Only when a weight presses down, uncomfortably tightly, on my face and the sides of my head, do I sit up against Monadofy's gate. My physical sight has gone dark.

Confusion and panic fail to consume me, though. Instead, my hands trail my face, finding my jacket, tied around my head to cover my eyes.

Cautiously, I lift the jacket, only to make another discovery. I can't hear the sounds of the cloth sliding between my fingers. It only takes a second for me to locate my burner phone, nestled on my lap, my earphones plugged into it, playing a YouTube video of white noise.

All at once, I relax. My breaths deepen. My headache remains, but my mind clears.

Sitting up straighter, I reapply the makeshift blindfold and lower the volume slightly. I close my eyes. Just as my future selves deduced, the sensory deprivation masks external stimuli, opening my mind to new possibilities.

Suddenly, an image forms before me, with equal depth, color, and texture as the real place.

A bedroom, with a curtained window, installed behind a desk, flush against a wall, with an open bedroom door beside it.

What's new to me, though, is the hallway beyond it. In one direction, I see the kitchen entrance. The other end contains doors I've never seen before, to the rest of the house.

4:40 PM

A minute of reading my notifications, head cocked to the side, listening for the slam of our metal kitchen screen door opening, before I lay back down. "I know you're worried, dude." I sigh, rereading Mode's messages on my phone's lock screen. "But what do I even tell you? Nothing's changed. And I can't do this forever.

"I just have to survive till tonight."

I reread his messages again, the ache of guilt slowly rising from within.

Mode

Today at 3:55 PM

Are you okay? You haven't posted in a while.

Today at 3:55 PM

I know you wouldn't do this if you didn't know what you were doing.

Today at 3:55 PM

You aren't going through this alone. I hope you feel that.

Today at 3:56 PM

You have me. Whatever you need, just ask.

Today at 3:56 PM

I'll make it happen.

"This guy also knows you exist so even if you tried to help, he'd... ."

I sigh. I turn my phone volume down again and resume my preferred sleeping position. After one last check, to confirm that my dagger is within reach, I relax and close my eyes.

I don't know how long I sleep again, or how long it takes for the sound to become noticeable. However, when it becomes loud and frequent enough, I recognize it immediately. Never mind that I haven't heard it in years.

In college, at most, I printed out one large research paper per class per quarter. Sometimes, to ensure that the printer worked properly, I plugged it into my laptop via USB cable, instead of relying on wi-fi. Dad tied the printer cable to the metal shelf housing the printer with a Velcro strap. When not in use, the cable would dangle off one of the shelf's support poles and onto the floor.

It's the sound of the metal USB cable tapping against wood.

The printer's shelf stands on the floor, next to a carpet. The carpet isn't large enough to reach the main door. The cable isn't long enough to reach the wood floor next to the door, either.

Any semblance of sleep vanishes.

In my right hand, I grip my phone, my thumb resting on the lock button, ready to mash it five times to call the police. In my other hand, I clench the dagger in a reverse grip: A fist locked around the hilt, my thumb covering the pommel, orienting the dagger's point downward, primed for stabbing. Jolting to my feet, I throw open the door between my chosen saferoom and Dad's office.

"Get out you fucker!"

The sound stops.

Ready to stab this asshole to death, I wait: For his swift footsteps, for him to touch me, for the click of a gun's safety, for the swishing of a knife, but none of those things happens. Instead, the tapping of the object—that can't be the USB printer cable against the wood floor—resumes, except it approaches me, sliding along the carpet between taps. It stops, inches from my bare feet.

Stepping back, I'm poised to retreat back in to my saferoom and slam the office door shut with my elbow and shoulder, but before I can, the tapping resumes. Plastic—

Plastic, not metal, first taps against, then slides along, metal, jarring my arm—

I startle and drop the dagger. Now, an object—

No.

My right hand, now free of my phone, examines the object: An unmoving, floating, plastic USB flash drive.

4:50 PM

I know what to do, so it takes me both more and less time to see what I want to see. It takes less time, because there are plenty of photos of Monadofy online. Once I can see at her height, my mental point of view expands accordingly.

It takes more time to see what I want, because I don't want anyone to notice anything. My attempts at projecting alternate memories over the house flash by, riddled with dozens of single-point failures.

When I fail, she calls the police.

Either that, I receive a knife—

No.

That wasn't a knife I saw, at the park.

It was a dagger.

Sometimes, I receive a dagger in my chest, throat, and eyes, in quick succession.

The scope of my vision widens. I thoroughly scan the property, to ensure my hybrid, telepathic and technopathic projections are perfect: To fool passersby and Monadofy's security cameras in the trash. Whatever I can't see from the front, I gather from Google Street View and real estate websites.

Sensory deprivation provides me what the Internet can't.

The imminent, cool relief of Monadofy's own tap water running down my throat and face, reinvigorates me long enough to reach my goal.

I afford myself a smile.

Without getting up, I tilt my head to one side and silently unlock the gate and front door from the inside. Only by correcting my failures to muffle the front door scratching against the doormat, and my footsteps against the hardwood, does my plan succeed.

I physically confirm the location of the office door, and repeatedly narrow my consciousness' focus, until I see the office itself.

Empowered by my dimensional and temporal doppelgangers alongside me, I silently and telekinetically lift the recliner up and away from the door, nudge it open, and slip the flash drive inside.

All it takes is a few taps against the floor, and Monadofy does exactly what I wanted, want, and will want, her to do.

I can see her in real time, now.

No speculation.

No guesswork.

No bullshit.

Another phase of my plan complete, I lean against her

kitchen island, water dripping off my face and arms onto the tile. I watch, hear, and share in Monadofy's feelings and actions. I shake with excitement, not fear, as my hands and fingers mimic hers.

Monadofy

Today at 5:10 PM

> He's here

Today at 5:10 PM

> He gave me a usb in dad's office with PLAY ME on it

Today at 5:11 PM

> He didn't touch me and I didn't hear him come in

Today at 5:11 PM

> Because it was floating

5:12 PM

That's it. I don't care if I get shot on sight or go to—

No.

I do care if I'm shot on sight, or go to the psych ward. Everyone has to know I'm not crazy, that I didn't make anything up, just to lure officers here to murder them. I'm not on drugs—

I'm not on illegal drugs.

I must explain that I confirmed he was a home invader before doing anything, didn't leave the house to fight him, and did everything I could to stop him from going onto my property. Laptop, iPhone, dagger, landline phone, and brailled flash drive in my arms, I haul ass into the bathroom and lock the door. Turning on the shower, I sit facing the door and muffle the landline phone's back speaker with a folded towel. Phone pressed to my ear, volume turned nearly all the way down, and dagger held in reverse-grip in my left hand, I make the call

"911. What's your emergency?"

I answer by harnessing fifteen to twenty years of watching breaking news.

"He's in my house. I'm blind so I don't know what he looks like. He hacked my laptop and phone so I'm calling on my landline. I turned on the shower so he can't hear me." A twinge of doubt seeps through, before I can resist: "I think."

"Can you confirm your address for me?" *She believes me. Thank fuck.*

I can't suppress my panic. "I don't want him to hear me."

"You're otherwise alone?" she asks, faster than before.

"My parents left this morning."

"When?"

"Seven."

"Where are they now?"

I strain to listen for any signs that he knows where I am, and that I'm on the phone. "They won't get home in time."

A firm request: "Stay on the line okay? We know what to do."

"Mm-hmmm."

An acknowledging sound that I hope she heard, as I set down the landline phone on the carpet, on top of the folded towel. I grab my earphones, plugged into my laptop, put one earbud in, and set down the dagger. "Sixty-six percent battery power," announces my screen reader, before I remove the earbud again.

"Hello?"

I perk up, holding the landline to my ear, and pointing the dagger at the closed door. "Hmm?"

"Police are on their way. Until then is there anything else you can tell us?"

It takes all my willpower to suppress my relieved sigh.

"Thank you. He knows we have security cameras. But he probably—He broke them by now."

"Do you know where they are?"

"Outside."

"When did he get there?"

I make a verbal shrug noise. "He first rang the doorbell after lunch but I bet he was there before then."

"Officers are almost there. Don't come out unless one identifies themselves."

"Yeah," I affirm.

"Can you tell us where you keep the spare key?"

Kicking myself profusely: "Shit—I wish I could but I can't."

Simultaneously: "She can't."

I continue explaining: "I don't have a spare key I think."

Again, simultaneously: "She doesn't have a spare key. She thinks."

The 911 operator asks one question, in a hushed voice, completely different from her previous tone. "Who's there?"

Sitting completely still, hoping I'm not hearing things, he answers for me, with a familiar, high, clear laugh.

At a faster pace, the operator doesn't wait for him to finish before reporting, "Police are a minute away from her—"

"If that's what you want to think."

The killer continues to speak through the phone in my hand and from all around me, his voice as clear as if he was speaking in my ear. "Don't bother. Everyone from both departments can hear me."

The flash drive ascends past my scrabbling hands, before grazing the edge of my left ear. "Neither of them will get here in time."

5:17 PM

Positioning myself is low-risk. She won't expect me to stand here, because if she saw someone doing it in a movie, let alone in broad daylight?

She'd call them an idiot.

My plan takes all my mental energy, though. Now, only Monadofy's face, and the house's doorways and hallways, stay in focus.

As frustrating as she's made this for me? Even after all I've seen, see, felt, and feel? Getting here was worth it.

She's made this much more fun.

 Today at 5:17 PM

You were doomed as soon as I got here.

We both know how this ends.

Today at 5:17 PM

You were doomed as soon as I got here.

Today at 5:17 PM

I'll show you exactly what I can do.

Today at 5:17 PM

So now?

Today at 5:17 PM

Fuck the rules.

Today at 5:17 PM

I want to have some fun.

Today at 5:17 PM

I'll be right back.

I create this projection easily. The neighbors won't care if a cop car drives by, as long as it's not giving chase. Hell, even a cop knocking on Monadofy's door is fine, as long as she doesn't resist.

Which she won't.

The hard part is deciding how, exactly, I want to break the projection. As I've experienced before, one well-placed attack would kill me.

The outcomes solidify as I creep into position. In each outcome, I mask my footsteps, so I can stealth my target freely. In each outcome, I maintain the illusion for everyone except my target.

In each outcome, I retrieve the small, serrated knife from Monadofy's kitchen at my side, telekinetically stabbing my first target in the spine. Empowered by the force from dozens of hands striking the same blow, I cut the target's spinal cord, leaving the officer's bulletproof vest and protective gear mostly intact.

It's easy to single out the rest, lay their bodies in their patrol car, parked outside Monadofy's home, and project my last illusion.

Eyes burning into the bodies from all angles, motions growing more practiced by the second, I paint blood on the door handles, windows, and the asphalt—even my own, drawn from another slash on my arm.

A single image overtakes me: The exact same street, sans the car.

I brim with the glucose and ATP stored in the cops' blood and organs, and the chemical energy from the car's battery and gasoline. The neural connections enabling the cops' senses, storing their memories, and encoding their knowledge, become mine.

This time, I've vanished the evidence, without squandering the resources before me in a furious crash.

What I gave you is real, and you know it.

I won't kill you, and you know it.

Because if I did?

You couldn't play my Inscryption mod.

5:45 PM

Her account still rings in my ears as I take my first shaky steps out of the bathroom. Squeezing past the recliner, pulling open the office door, and returning to my room, laptop and USB keyboard tucked under my arm, I still clutch my dagger in my free hand. After a couple trips, I've reverted the house back to how it appeared when my parents left.

Only then, do I finally plug the flash drive into my computer, on the lookout for signs that I downloaded a virus. As I do, I finally open Entropy again.

Monadofy

Today at 5:52 PM

Officers apprehended the suspect outside my home.

Today at 5:52 PM

After a short pursuit on foot, he failed to comply with their requests to put his hands up.

Today at 5:52 PM

He attempted to assault them with a knife.

Today at 5:52 PM

The chief of the police station closest to my house confirmed the suspect carried several phones with the apps I described.

Today at 5:53 PM

And evidence of the surveillance and stalking I described.

Today at 5:53 PM

Someone will contact me if there are any developments.

Today at 5:53 PM

That's what the 911 operator told me.

Today at 5:53 PM

They stopped him just in time.

Mode

Today at 5:54 PM

THANK FUCK

Today at 5:54 PM

Any idea of a motive?

Monadofy

Today at 5:55 PM

No.

Today at 5:55 PM

But I have ideas.

Mode

Today at 5:55 PM

Like?

Monadofy

Today at 5:55 PM

Like this guy in Alaska who made killing his victims into a game.

Today at 5:55 PM

Hunting them out in the wild.

Today at 5:55 PM

But that was in the middle of nowhere.

Today at 5:55 PM

And he targeted people no one would miss if they were dead.

Today at 5:55 PM

> This was premeditated in the same way, but it was urban.

Today at 5:55 PM

> So he gave me Ready or Not vibes—or maybe more like Hush.

Today at 5:56 PM

> Calling this fun but

Today at 5:56 PM

> Or maybe he didn't mean "fun" like that.

Mode

Today at 5:57 PM

> He sent you Undertale sound files. So of course he knew you knew about Undertale's easter eggs. Like the FUN value.

Monadofy

Today at 5:56 PM

> And he was forensically aware 'cause he knew about our home security

Today at 5:56 PM

> And he wouldn't have touched the flash drive—that's why it floated.

Today at 5:56 PM

> Hell—I bet he didn't even before he brought it in.

Mode

Today at 5:56 PM

> EXACTLY.

Today at 5:56 PM

> Do they know what he looks like?

Monadofy

Today at 5:57 PM

> No.

Today at 5:57 PM

Well kinda?

Today at 5:57 PM

They didn't find any pictures of him on his phones.

Mode

Today at 5:57 PM

And I'm assuming they haven't told you if they did a reverse image search or have surveillance footage.

Monadofy

Today at 5:57 PM

They said they don't have any.

Mode

Today at 5:57 PM

Body cam footage?

Monadofy

Today at 5:57 PM

That too.

Mode

Today at 5:57 PM

I'm not surprised.

Monadofy

Today at 5:58 PM

Why?

Mode

Today at 5:58 PM

But do they have witnesses?

Monadofy

Today at 5:58 PM

Don't know.

Mode

Today at 5:58 PM

So no.

Today at 5:59 PM

Do they have a description?

Monadofy

Today at 5:59 PM

There's drawings but they couldn't agree what he looked like.

Mode

Today at 6:00 PM

Did he have a getaway car?

Monadofy

Today at 6:00 PM

No why?

Mode

Today at 6:00 PM

Do they know his name at least?

Monadofy

Today at 6:01 PM

Dude I don't know!

Today at 6:01 PM

They couldn't find his name anywhere not even in his apps.

Mode

Today at 6:01 PM

His posts.

Monadofy

Today at 6:01 PM

Mm-hmmm.

Mode

Today at 6:01 PM

And he doesn't even have fingerprints.

Today at 6:01 PM

When is your aunt supposed to get there?

Monadofy

Today at 6:01 PM

Don't know but it's supposed to be seven-ish?

Today at 6:02 PM

Tangent—plugged in the flash drive a couple minutes ago.

Mode

Today at 6:02 PM

So you hid it from the cops.

Monadofy

Today at 6:02 PM

They wouldn't understand.

Today at 6:02 PM

They'd think I was crazy.

Mode

Today at 6:02 PM

True.

Monadofy

Today at 6:02 PM

He wanted to kill me but he wanted to have FUN with it first.

Today at 6:03 PM

The braille was for me—it was 3D-printed on.

Today at 6:04 PM

The only way he could've made it more obvious was if he brailled a microcassette tape.

Mode

Today at 6:04 PM

> Or floppy disc.

Today at 6:04 PM

> Or there's a virus on it but it's for them not you.

Today at 6:05 PM

> So he can track them.

Today at 6:05 PPM

> And kill them too.

Monadofy

Today at 6:05 PM

> Hadn't thought of that.

Today at 6:05 PM

> Wait what do you mean them too?

Mode

Today at 6:06 PM

> Keep me posted okay?

Monadofy

Today at 6:06 PM

> Yeah.

Today at 6:06 PM

> Gonna start looking at it for real after getting food.

Today at 6:06 PM

> Be back after dinner.

Now that I've finished recounting the 911 operator's statements, I finally box the dagger above my desk where it belongs. It takes all my willpower to have dinner like I promised, rather than immediately digging through the files, but I do so. I'm so excited that I don't even put my dishes in the sink.

The flash drive contains only two files: A Slay the Spire

mod file, and a word doc named identically to the flash drive, and the text brailled via 3D printing onto the other side: 'ARCANE_ARCHIVE'. Just to make sure, I check the file name, and it's spelled exactly how I think it's spelled. One character at a time, I scroll over the name with my screen reader. 'ARCANE_ARCHIVE' is in all-caps, with an underscore between the words, instead of a space. I giggle. "At least if you were going to reference endgame spoilers, then go all the way... ."

I open the file. Before reading it, I set the cursor on the first word, and perform the key command that reads the word's formatting information aloud.

"Seventeen point. White on black. Determination. Normal style. Line spacing: One lines. Paragraph formatting. Aligned left. Outline level: Body text."

Gamemaster.jar is a Slay the Spire mod that adds new enemies, events, bosses, and relics, among other things. The exact changes will depend on the character you use. It also has compatibility with lots of other character and content mods. Even ones you don't have.

But let's be real here. You wanna play this 'cause it changes the story. Meaning that it adds one. Because now, Slay the Spire is written and narrated like the best part of Inscryption. And I don't just mean the campaign at the table. And yes: the puzzles are compatible with NVDA. And aren't a pain in the ass. And there's some extra special stuff when you play Gamemaster with your own Inscryption-based mod activated. I won't give anything away, though.

The installation process is easy: I just have to copy the Gamemaster mod into the appropriate folder, open Slay the Spire, and check Gamemaster's box in the mod selection screen. When the game loads, I notice the extent of the changes immediately: Instead of the usual main menu music, static—

NO.

Static, mixed to ebb and flow like the ocean, plays instead. After several seconds, my screen reader announces: "Press any button to start," and I oblige.

The new interface and nomenclature on the menu screen are exactly how I remember them, from both source games. Once I've found the New Game button, this time free of glitches, I send brief, but excited, Entropy messages.

Monadofy

Today at 6:30 PM

DUDE IT WORKS IT ACTUALLY WORKS EEEEE!!!

Mode

Today at 6:30 PM

So your laptop's okay.

Monadofy

Today at 6:30 PM

Yeah.

Mode

Today at 6:30 PM

THANK FUCK

Monadofy

Today at 6:30 PM

The mod's called Gamemaster. It's ridonculous.

Mode

Today at 6:31 PM

How do you know?

Monadofy

Today at 6:31 PM

> I got a readme with the mod.

Today at 6:31 PM

> Attaching it now if you want it.

Mode

Today at 6:31 PM

> YES PLEASE

Monadofy

Today at 6:31 PM

> Okay here.

Today at 6:31 PM

> ARCANE_ARCHIVE.docx
>
> 17 kB

Mode

Today at 6:31 PM

> Reading it now.

Today at 6:32 PM

> Is it voiced?

Monadofy

Today at 6:32 PM

> What?

Mode

Today at 6:32 PM

> Is Gamemaster voiced?

Monadofy

Today at 6:32 Pm

> Don't know—haven't started yet.

Today at 6:32 PM

> Just figured out what the menu looks like.

Today at 6:32 PM

> Don't think it is though.

Today at 6:33 PM

> It's screen-reader compatible. NVDA already reads the text aloud…

Today at 6:33 PM

> If it was voiced it'd just get in the way.

Today at 6:33 PM

> Starting a run with one of the base game characters.

Mode

Today at 6:33 PM

> Can I have the mod?

Monadofy

Today at 6:33 PM

> It probly won't fit. Seems like it'd be big.

Today at 6:34 PM

> Gamemaster.jar
>
> 16.66 MB

Today at 6:34 PM

> Run's starting now

Today at 6:34 PM

> HOLY SHIT IT'S AUDIO DESCRIBED.

Mode

Today at 6:34 PM

> So he meant it.

Today at 6:34 PM

> He really made it.

Today at 6:34 PM

> He's probably responding to things in real time but…

Monadofy

Today at 6:34 PM

> HOLY FUCK THERE'S VOICE ACTING.

Today at 6:35 PM

> But only you've heard this voice and I don't think—SHIT WHAT'S HIS NAME?

Today at 6:35 PM

> MICHAEL WINCOTT

Today at 6:36 PM

> Michael Wincott—I don't think he's a gamer but ehh.

Today at 6:36 PM

> It's probly just a guy who sounds like him but I don't care.

Today at 6:36 PM

> LET'S DO THIS. BRB.

I shouldn't feel surprised over how my first run ends, but I am anyway. My excitement to encounter each map's boss completely overshadows the necessity to solve the puzzles away from the table. I progressed through the run "too fast," and neared the end "too soon". However, against all my gamer instincts, I look forward to dying, because I have the chance to make the "perfect memento" representing my first run. I don't skip or ignore text, even as my session reaches, then exceeds, an hour long. I save scum as little as possible. I even name one of my cards after Michael Wincott, despite questioning his dubious gaming status to myself.

"No. He isn't one. Do I go cold, or does my heart skip a beat? He hasn't played it. Not the one you know, anyway."

He's speaking from beside me, and all around me.

"And yes: The office door wasn't supposed to be open." He's calm, casual, and familiar. "And yes: I pushed that chair away from it. "So the flash drive would fit."

A thud on my desk, inches from my laptop, laying me open. I all but jump out of my seat, but the slight grind of glass on wood soon pins me down. It's a slick, cold glass, resting against my right palm. The familiar scent of my favorite liquor wafts up from it, mixed with hot chocolate. As I pick it up, ice clinks in the glass.

From behind me, in the nearest corner of my room, I hear the same clinking sound. Even as I shoot my hand to one side, fumbling for my phone, its voiceover starts talking from behind me—

No.

Floating beside my right ear, its screen bumping against the side of my head and neck, it begins to speak my passcode, one character at a time, while he takes a small sip of his drink.

Without any hesitation, I down my glass.

He doesn't force me to call anyone or post anything. He doesn't force me to text my parents, telling them everything's normal. He opens my settings, nonverbally confirming that my wi-fi is on, and my Bluetooth is off, just as I intended. My phone isn't connected to any unfamiliar devices, my location services are still deactivated, and my apps' data access permissions, password, and fingerprint usages are unchanged.

Lastly, he opens my online banking app. Without either of us moving, he logs in, with my preexisting credentials, lingers on the app's home screen for a moment, then closes it.

Seemingly satisfied, he telekinetically sets my phone on my desk, rises from the floor, and strides over to me. He rotates my chair, also without touching it, so I face him. It tilts up and backward slightly, but not enough to unbalance me.

When I rise, as if in response, he firmly places my right

hand over his shoulder. Under my palm, a patch of his jacket tears?

No.

It liquifies—

No.

It bleeds.

It bleeds, fibers contorted into droplets, compelled to smell like iron, and cling to my hand, if only for a moment. Even as the exposed, underlying fabric of his T-shirt brushes my skin, he presses a small knife into my left hand, its hilt sticky with blood. He even perfects my reverse grip.

Briefly lifting my right hand from his shoulder, he guides the knife's tip so it's in the center of the opening: Over his left brachial artery. He even applies slight pressure on it.

I don't push further.

As it makes contact, my left arm spasms, stabbing forward and downward at the indicated spot, while the rest of me remains completely still. Instead of wielding the combat knife, my hand grips a—

A kitchen knife, with a short, thin blade and simple, wooden handle.

The knife formerly owned by law enforcement stays in the positions he demonstrated for an instant longer, so the vision to sink in. Shaking as the illusory blood splatters onto me, I withdraw my arm and easily secure it in the sheath that levitates toward me. He turns my chair back toward my computer. I sit again.

Next, the click of a long, skinny object lands in my lap. In one moment, a seasoned hand slides the police baton into a sheath on a belt. In the next, the same hand grabs for the same baton, but fails to do so in time. With the same kitchen knife, he first severs the officer's spinal cord, paralyzing them, then penetrates first one lung, then the other.

Testing the weight of the police baton in my left hand, its grip conforms with mine, the material firm, pliable, and somehow, pulsing regularly, as if breathing.

A small giggle from behind me. "It's nylon. But close enough."

The last object drapes over my lap: A Kevlar vest, specifications changed to suit me. Only slight tearing in its lower half remains from its previous owner: Remnants of their exsanguination, caused by stab wounds to their liver and femoral artery.

Donning the vest, I turn my head toward him. He's making an Entropy call, but the dial tone isn't the same. Its lower audio quality, due to lower sampling rate, emulates an early 2000s mobile phone. Regardless, I recognize it immediately. Mode's even, unsurprised tone on the other end of the call, only confirms it.

"You didn't need to change that."

The same small giggle: "I know. But I wanted to. And besides. We both know, I didn't have to make the ringtone audible. I could even video call you without her phone. And you'd answer."

The sounds of shattering glass and fragmented metal emanates from both ends of the call. An unfamiliar phone drops into my hand for an instant, before hurling into the air toward me, but even as I brace for impact, it doesn't break against my skull. Instead, the burner phone dissolves—

No.

It too, bleeds, its fragments transforming into buckets of blood, pouring over my body, far more than contained by three, four, five, six, more, people.

He grips my shoulder and turns my chair backwards as the digital blood dries, or rather, evaporates off of me.

I open my eyes.

A pair of muted thuds impact the floor in front of me. I remove his hand from my shoulder.

I lean down toward Mode, who sits up and sets a packed bag on his lap. I hold my hands out for him. In sync, our breaths even out, and an utter lack of surprise passes between us. We switch places, so he sits in my chair, and I sit on the floor beside him.

Just as we exhale simultaneously, my phone emits a three-toned, bright sound: The normal text message receipt notification. In the same moment, the doorbell rings, several times in succession.

november

Please Pass the Turkey

Lauren Patzer

Hugo stormed into the tiny reception room at the institute, his wild wavy black hair bouncing with each step.

Becky Margle perked up as he passed near the front desk. She sat up straight and pushed out her chest. "Hi Hugo!" she shouted at him. "Any plans for Thanksgiving?"

Hugo stopped cold and stared at her with his dark, bushy eyebrows raised. "Solving world hunger, of course!" he announced, his thick Slavic accent pronounced by the loudness of his proclamation. The two people sitting in the waiting room lowered the magazines they were reading for a moment and then slowly raised them back up.

"Okay," Becky replied as she twirled a blonde hair absently on her left shoulder.

"Good day!" he shouted and Becky jumped. Hugo resumed his walk and passed through the secure facility door to Becky's right.

Becky sighed as the door clicked shut. She pressed the intercom button. "Mister Donovan, Doctor Gratavich has arrived," she said quietly.

"What?" a gruff voice responded. "Oh, right. Hugo."

Mister Donovan's sigh was audible over the intercom. "Very well. Thank you, Miss Margle."

"A pleasure to serve you, sir," she replied and lifted her finger from the button. She made a sour face.

Hugo removed his heavy coat and tossed it on a chair near a locker to the right of the laboratory door. The lights came on automatically sensing movement and Hugo strode quickly to center one of three long benches arrayed with equipment. He rolled up his white shirt sleeves, turned on a computer screen and began typing on the keyboard. He paused for a moment and looked around the room. He scowled at the absence of anyone else and turned his attention back to the computer.

Mister Donovan, dressed in a grey suit with a blue and red tie, entered the room and immediately plastered a fake smile on his face when he saw Hugo. Hugo didn't turn around. Mister Donovan cleared his throat.

Hugo ignored him for a moment and then gave him a passing glance. "Ahh, Mister Donovan," Hugo said gruffly. "Where's my new assistant?"

Mister Donovan's smile faded a moment before he blinked and reinforced it even harder. "Doctor Gratavich, we've had some trouble replacing the three assistants you fired over the last month. Perhaps it's just the holidays causing the issue."

"Try harder. Isn't that what you're paid for?" Hugo looked at his computer screen and didn't even glance at Mister Donovan.

"Ahem, yes, well, about what people are paid for—how's the nanotransistor research coming along? We haven't had updates on the project in over a month."

Hugo stopped typing and scrunched up his eyes. "I told you the avian growth research is vitally important!"

"Doctor Gratavich, we're contracted to provide an improved nanotransistor to the military within six months. That's the nanotechnology work you were hired for."

"What about humanity?!" Hugo shouted. He turned around and fixed Mister Donovan with his stare. "Eight hundred million people go to bed hungry everyday! Do you know how many die from starvation?"

"I understand," Mister Donovan replied. "But do you really think improving the size of turkeys is going to solve world hunger? Wouldn't crop yield improvement or something be better?"

"Don't you care about people?!" Hugo hollered.

"Well, of course, I do, but the nanotransistor project takes precedent," Mister Donovan replied. "We allowed for a small percentage of your budget to go to a side project per our employment agreement, but it's taken up entirely too much time and resources."

"People will die if I don't finish this!" Hugo replied. He slammed his fist on the counter. "I could finish that insignificant nanotransistor work in a week! But it won't save any lives—it will only cost lives!"

"A week, you say?" Mister Donovan smiled. "Good. I'll expect some results on the nanotransistor project within a week or your contract here is terminated."

"Just get me my assistant!" Hugo shouted as he took a step toward Mister Donovan, who involuntarily stepped backward and bumped into a counter.

"You have a week, Hugo," Mister Donovan said, turned around quickly and left the room.

Hugo scowled at the retreating executive. As the door shut and the relative silence returned to the room, Hugo sighed.

He looked around the room at the beakers and small vats sitting on the tables and shook his head.

"Stupid nanotransistor," Hugo mumbled. He closed the file on avian growth serum and opened his nanotransistor folder.

Friday morning, Hugo walked into Mister Donovan's office and smiled grimly at the executive sitting behind his giant walnut desk.

"Your nanotransistor redesign was delivered…and I still don't have an assistant," Hugo said.

Mister Donovan clicked a few times on his computer and nodded.

"Your redesign work is just what we were looking for. It's been delivered to the military and they're happy with the results," he said and gave Hugo a thumbs up.

"Wonderful," Hugo replied with a strained smile. "My assistant?"

"Ahh yes, your assistant is no longer required. We're buying out the remainder of your contract. You can clean out your avian growth experimental materials by the end of the day. We no longer require your services."

"What?" Hugo's eyes went wide and he was shocked. "My contract clearly states both lines of research are authorized and—"

"We've bought out the remaining nine months of your current contract. The money will be deposited within the hour. The company has changed direction. You're no longer needed, Doctor Gratavich. If we have future need for your services, we'll be in touch. Thank you for your contributions to nanotransistor technology."

Hugo opened his mouth to speak, but found he had

nothing further to contribute. He simply turned and walked out the door.

As he walked back across the lobby, Becky rushed out from behind the desk and got in front of Hugo. "Hugo," she said as she stepped in front of him. "I heard about them letting you go and I'm so sorry."

Hugo stopped and looked at her with a blank look on his face. "Uh, thank you. I'm not sure how I'm going to complete my avian growth research now," Hugo mumbled.

"Oh, I can help you!" Becky replied. "I've got a degree in biology with a specialty in avian biology!"

"What?" Hugo took a step back and looked at Becky as if for the first time. "Why didn't you put in your paperwork to be my assistant?"

"Oh that," Becky smiled shyly. "I tried, but Mister Donovan wasn't having any of it. He didn't think your project would go anywhere, but I've seen some of your research and I think you're on the right track."

"Really?" Hugo said with a frown. "How do you think we can get by the mass inversion problem?"

"I'm pretty sure you just need a quantum mass exchanger, probably suspended in a subatomic matrix keyed to the avian cell." Becky winked. "I've already worked up a serum additive to try. I'll bring it along to your place Saturday."

"Well, Miss Margle, I look forward to our collaboration this weekend," Hugo replied with a genuine smile.

"Oh, so do I, but please call me Becky," she replied with a giggle and then walked with a little swing in her hips back behind the reception desk.

Hugo watched her walk back with eyebrows raised. He swallowed nervously. He wasn't sure where his excitement was coming from, but he felt a rare stirring in his loins. He quickly cleared his throat and walked to the security door.

Hugo stirred from his bed at the ringing of his doorbell. He jumped up and looked at the clock by the bedside. It was nearly 11am. He'd been up late into the night transferring equipment and opening new boxes in his basement to setup his lab.

He threw on a robe over his naked self and ran down the stairs to the front door. He opened and gasped. Becky smiled at him as she held a satchel, but the amazing thing was her transformation from buttoned up receptionist to the wildly dressed Goth chick standing before him. She had earrings with strange symbols hanging from them and an upside down pentagram printed in red on her black t-shirt. She had a ring on every finger, each one a different design. Her face was made up darker including some very dark eye shadow applied thickly. Her long flowing blonde hair was tied up in a bun with what looked like black briar branches. The overall effect took his breath away and he temporarily forgot to hold his robe shut.

Becky looked down and winked. "Still got a little morning, uh, flora going on?"

"What?" Hugo asked and then looked down. He quickly shut his robe.

"Uh, my apologies. I just awoke. I will go make myself presentable," he said and waved her into the house.

"You're presentable now, depending on what you have in mind," Becky said as she walked by him and gently brushed her hand against his stubbly cheek.

"Yes, uh," Hugo mumbled and shook his head. "Research before, uh, pleasure."

As Becky sat down on the couch in the sparsely furnished

living room, Hugo quickly shut the front door and rushed back up the stairs.

Becky turned to watch him go and smiled. She retrieved a small perfume vial from her satchel marked "Musk" and lightly dabbed it on her bare shoulders exposed by two cutouts in the black t-shirt.

"Too easy," she whispered triumphantly.

Upstairs, Hugo pulled on some clothes quickly and rushed into the bathroom. He looked at his flushed face in the mirror and frowned. "What is wrong with you?" he whispered at his reflection. "You are not a pimply schoolboy! Pull yourself together."

He ran a brush through his unruly hair and brought it to some semblance of order. He grabbed his electric razor and scoured the stubble from his face. He quickly brushed his teeth and dabbed a bit of cologne on his neck. He stopped mid dab and scowled at himself. "What are you doing? Get on with your research, you fool!" he growled at his reflection. He put the cologne down and walked out of the bathroom.

As he came down the stairs, the smell of eggs and bacon reached his nose and he gasped. He stepped quickly into the kitchen and saw Becky cooking up a full breakfast for the two of them. She even had the coffee pot brewing and Hugo was literally dumbstruck. Becky turned to him and smiled.

"Oh, I hope you don't mind," she said as she turned over the bacon. "It's hard to do good research on an empty stomach and without any coffee."

"Uh," Hugo mumbled.

"Well, you did say you just woke up, right?"

Hugo nodded.

Becky stepped back from the stove quickly and put her

hands to her cheeks.

"Oh, I'm so sorry! I totally invaded your space without asking! I just thought this would be quicker," she said and seemed truly mortified to have overstepped her bounds. Her dismay seemed to break through Hugo's befuddled mind and he strode up to her quickly.

"It's okay," he said reassuringly. "It's just been so long since anyone has worried about taking care of my needs that it's a little... surprising. Thank you, I would love to have some breakfast."

"Really?" she asked hesitantly.

Hugo nodded and her demeanor changed in an instant to a giddy schoolgirl rushing around the kitchen like a whirligig. She quickly lay out the plates laden with food, poured two glasses of orange juice, two cups of coffee and sat next to him with an ear to ear grin that had Hugo uncharacteristically smiling as well. The meal was going fine until half way through; there was a sharp knock at the door.

Hugo frowned. He didn't notice Becky rolling her eyes. Hugo got up from the table. The pounding on the door renewed with more urgency.

"Doctor Hugo Gratavich, this is the police!" a deep voice announced from the other side on the front door. Hugo gasped and jumped up. Becky looked annoyed, set her utensils down gently and picked up a napkin.

Hugo looked out the peephole and saw three uniformed policemen on his porch. In the background, three police cruisers were pulled up to his sidewalk with additional police standing by them. Becky dabbed the sides of her mouth with the napkin.

Hugo opened the door. "What is the problem, officers?" Hugo asked.

"Russian," the officer furthest from the door murmured. "That explains a lot."

"Wilkins," the officer in front of Hugo hissed as he turned to look at his fellow officer.

"I'm from the Czech Republic," Hugo responded. "I'm not Russian."

"It's immaterial, Doctor Gratavich," the officer in front said as he turned back to him. "We need you to come with us."

"But why?" Hugo said. "I've done nothing wrong."

"We've had some… occurrences downtown. We have come to understand it may be related to your research. Your employer was kind enough to give us your address."

"Former employer," Hugo replied. He folded his arms. "I've been here since I cleared out my office yesterday. What is the nature of the occurrences?"

"There have been some incidents related to your, umm, animal growth experiments," the officer replied. Hugo peered at his badge and saw the name 'Hopper.'

"Officer Hopper, am I under arrest?" Hugo asked.

The officer looked down and shook his head. "We strongly suggest you come with us, but you are not under arrest and you are not required to come with us," Officer Hopper said.

"Why do you have three police vehicles and all these policemen then?" Hugo asked.

"If you would come with us, you'll see why we took the precautions. Umm, do you have any experiments active on the premises?" The two officers behind Hopper stepped back involuntarily.

"No, I…" Hugo looked at the policemen and shook his head. "All my experiments have been done virtually and within the confines of a Petri dish. They could hardly be dangerous. I'm not even working with any controlled substances."

"Of course," Officer Hopper replied. "You could drive yourself if you like. We request you accompany us to one of our police warehouses next to police headquarters. We'll give you a police escort."

Hugo looked around at the officers and frowned. "All right, let me grab my coat and keys," Hugo said and stepped behind the front door to retrieve his coat and pulled his keys from the hook.

"I'll clean up in here, Hugo!" Becky shouted. Hugo turned and nodded absently.

"I will see you soon," Hugo replied to Becky and stepped out of the house.

As soon as the door shut, Becky stood up and looked down at the half-eaten food. "Such a waste, but it will hardly matter soon," she whispered. She walked to the window and watched Hugo pull out of the driveway in his plain brown sedan, following one police car, tightly pursued by the other two.

Becky smiled.

Hugo pulled into a fenced parking lot surrounding a large warehouse. He glanced to his left and saw the looming presence of town hall two blocks away; the large clock in the clock tower there read 2:15pm. He parked his car next to the lead police vehicle and turned it off. Several uniformed and plainclothes police peered into one of the open garage doors.

Officer Hopper met him as he stepped out of his car. "Doctor, it's just this way," the officer said and lead Hugo through a small door leading to a set of offices inside the warehouse.

Hugo looked around the room at different sets of scientific equipment and recognized the setup was more geared toward forensic science than the complex subjects he worked on daily. Officer Hopper led him through the office to a second one that was more setup like a morgue than anything else. A woman with long black hair tied up in a bun dressed in a lab coat with her back to them worked on something on the metal counter in front of her.

"Doctor Patel, this is Doctor Gratavich," Officer Hopper said. She moved her head to glance at them and then turned back to her work.

"Great, another Frankenstein with delusions of grandeur," she huffed.

Officer Hopper turned to Hugo. "Doctor Frankenstein was—" the officer began.

"I know who Frankenstein is, officer. It's not the first time someone has shown their ignorance by making pointless accusations," Hugo replied.

Doctor Patel whirled around with a scalpel in her hand and fire in her eyes. "It's morons like you who can't leave nature to its normal processes. Whether it's GMOs, DNA alteration or shoving drugs into cows, it's always the same with you lot!" She set the scalpel down and pulled off her gloves. She dropped them in a biohazard waste bin and walked across the lab. She picked up a coffee cup and took a small sip.

Hugo pursed his lips and didn't say anything. His eyes were drawn to the specimen laid out of the metal surface where Doctor Patel had been just a few moments before. He slowly walked up to the creature and frowned. Laid out on the table was a long, very hairy body of an animal with leathery wings nearly two feet long. The wings were folded in but looked huge. The ears were incredibly large. The rear of the creature's skull looked like it had exploded, leaving blood, bone and brain matter strewn about the wound.

"This has the features of a fruit bat," Hugo said as he pulled on a pair of gloves. He used a pair of clamps to pull the head of the large creature up so he could observe the face. The concave nose with a spear of flesh pointing up on the face was unmistakable. "This is a macrotus californicus?"

He turned to Doctor Patel. "How did it get so big?" he asked.

"We were hoping you could tell us what you did to the leaf-nosed bat, Frank," Doctor Patel sneered. "Look in the brain. Use the black light and observe the pituitary."

Hugo reached over and grabbed a flashlight. He looked at the lighted end to see the filter clipped onto it. He turned it on and pointed the light into the exposed brain. A small amount of clearly foreign substance glowed green. He turned off the flashlight and set it down.

"I do not know what that substance is. Have you had it analyzed?" Hugo asked as he stepped back from the creature.

"These specimens just came in this morning. I haven't been able to tell what the substance is. It doesn't respond to any of the standard test strips, so a deeper analysis will be required," Doctor Patel said. She set her cup down and walked back over to Hugo and Officer Hopper. "So if you could just tell us what you injected directly into the bat's brain that would be helpful."

"I did no such thing. I haven't solved the mass inversion problem, although it seems whoever did this has. Besides, my test subject will be meleagris gallopavo, not a cave bat," Hugo said with a sniff.

"Turkeys?" Doctor Patel asked. Hugo nodded.

"You said 'will be,' is that correct, Doctor Gratavich?" Officer Hopper asked.

"My permit is very specific and I follow sound scientific methods," Hugo replied. "What use is growing a bat that you can't eat?"

"Well, that excuse doesn't get you out of suspicion entirely, Doctor," the policeman stated.

"What do you mean?" Hugo asked. He looked back and forth between Doctor Patel and the officer. "You said specimens, but I only see this bat."

Officer Hopper looked at Doctor Patel and she sighed. She waved her hand at another door. "This way," Officer Hopped said as he walked to the door Doctor Patel had waved at. Hugo followed him and the door opened onto the warehouse floor near the open garage door. Doctor Patel followed closely behind with her coffee in hand. A large animal lay on the cement floor, its skin was a mottled pink and purple with strange patterns on the flesh that appeared to be stretch marks. They approached from the rear of the animal.

"Well, I certainly wouldn't experiment on a hippopotamus." Hugo chuckled. "I'm not even sure what the scientific name is for it."

"It's not a hippopotamus amphibious, Frank," Doctor Patel said. "It's a cavia porcellus; definitely on the menu in certain countries."

Hugo laughed. He looked at his two escorts. "It has no hair, how can it be a guinea pig? Besides, it's enormous!" Hugo said.

As they approached the head, it had the same damage to the cranium that the bat exhibited. Hugo turned his head a bit to look at the wound.

"Some artifact of the abnormal growth prevented the hair follicles from keeping up with the other cells growing at an accelerated rate," Doctor Patel said.

"The unknown substance was also found in the brain?" Hugo asked as he looked at the gory wound.

"Yes, but the flesh at the back of the skull remained intact enough that we could identify a small injection site," Doctor Patel said.

"Aha!" Hugo scoffed. "Amateurs! You can't inject growth hormone or whatever it is directly into the brain. If it was that simple, every farmer would be doing it."

"What do you mean?" Doctor Patel asked.

"I developed a time release suspension that allows the growth catalyst to be delivered across the entire body via the blood stream, ensuring gradual and consistent exposure. That allows the subject to gradually increase its size over a short period of time. This prevents ruptures of the cells, organs, skin." Hugo pointed at the skull. "So you won't get this kind of result."

"Could someone be trying to steal your work?" Officer Hopper asked.

"Well, they're doing a poor job of it. My method is keyed very specifically to the meleagris gallopavo anatomy. It's not going to work on just any animal and certainly not injected directly into the brain."

"That doesn't make it any less dangerous to humanity," Doctor Patel said flatly.

"This is for humanity," Hugo argued. "Populations across the globe are suffering from starvation!"

"Just the same," Officer Hopper said. "I'm going to request an injunction on your scientific work until we can get this resolved."

"What?" Hugo screamed. "You can't do that! I didn't do this garbage science you see before you!"

"Looks like you're getting shut down, Frankenstein," Doctor Patel smirked and walked back into the office holding her cup of coffee in the air like a trophy.

Hugo scowled at Officer Hopper. "It's Saturday, right?" he asked the lawman.

"Yes," Officer Hopper replied.

"Probably won't get a judge to even look at this before Monday, correct?" Hugo asked.

"I suppose," Officer Hopper replied. "It doesn't really matter. Doctor overachiever in there already contacted the FBI. They'll probably confiscate everything before the ink dries on our injunction."

Hugo walked toward the open garage door.

"Hey!" Officer Hopper shouted.

"Am I under arrest?" Hugo said as he stopped and turned around.

"No, but you should stay here in case we have more questions."

"I only have two days to complete my work. You can ask me questions Monday," Hugo replied. He turned around and walked out the door.

Hugo parked in front of his house and ran to the front door where a note was stuck to the glass pane. He pulled the note off and read it.

I've taken your equipment. Come to the following address if you want to complete your work. Don't call the police or you'll lose precious time.

The note was signed Becky with a little heart next to her name.

"No!" Hugo shouted. He ran into the house and went

down the stairs to the basement. Some equipment remained, but the larger pieces were missing. He knew he couldn't get anything done without them. He visited his small refrigerator and noted the vials of his creation were missing as well. He looked at his watch and cursed. It was already three in the afternoon and he had less than forty-eight hours to complete his work before they tried to stop him.

He looked at the note and put the address into the mapping app on his phone. The address was two hours outside of town.

"I am in the rice!" Hugo cursed as he ran his hands through his hair. He ran up the stairs and out the front door without shutting it. He jumped into his brown sedan, started it up and pressed the accelerator to the floor. His car screeched away from the house.

Hugo pulled up outside a small cabin and his heart sunk. Becky stood in front of the cabin waving to him. He stopped his car and got out, cursing under his breath. As he stormed toward Becky, he was dismayed to see she was just as confident as when he left her earlier in the day.

"Becky, what have you done?" he demanded as he stopped in front of her.

"I've saved you," Becky said with a smile.

"What? My work is about to be stopped for who knows how many months and you've taken my equipment, wasting precious time!" Hugo shouted.

"Did you tell the police where you were going?" she asked slyly. Hugo shook his head.

"Why would I tell those vultures where I'm going?"

"Exactly." Becky nodded. "They just want to stop you. I

want to see you succeed."

"You have a very strange way of showing it," Hugo grumbled.

"Come with me—I have everything setup for you to continue your experiments away from the prying eyes of the government," Becky said and walked to the side of the cabin. Hugo followed her until they reached an all terrain vehicle. She climbed in and pointed to the passenger seat.

Hugo sighed and got in. "Where are we going?"

"We need to ditch your vehicle. They might have put a tracker on it," she said as she grabbed his leg and squeezed it lovingly. "I've got everything you need."

Becky started up the ATV. She pointed at the dashboard. "Put your cell phone in the compartment if you don't want them following us. It will block all signals."

Hugo pulled out his cell phone and hesitated for a moment. He looked at Becky and sighed. He put the phone in the compartment.

Becky pressed the gas and they drove into the forest.

After twenty minutes of zigzagging through the forest, they reached another road. Becky's small SUV waited there. She got out, retrieved her backpack from the rear of the ATV and walked to the SUV. Hugo shook his head and followed her.

"These spy shenanigans are unnecessary," Hugo said.

"I'm just trying to protect our work," Becky said.

"Our work?!" Hugo bristled and stopped walking. "What are you talking about? You're just an assistant!"

"Have you solved the matter inversion problem, Hugo?"

Hugo clenched his jaw. "Not yet," he said. "Why?"

"You've just seen my work," Becky replied.

"What?"

"The bat and the guinea pig. I've figured out how to get matter inversion to work, but I need your expertise to deliver it in a slower more methodical manner so the subjects don't... come to an early end."

"How did you do this? What compounds did you utilize?" Hugo's anger dissipated quickly in the presence of learning new technologies. His geek flag waved hard.

Becky walked up to Hugo and one whiff of her smell caused his Neanderthal brain to thrill—a beautiful woman with a scientific mind. It was almost too much for him; the hormonal response of his body confused him.

"Let's test it before we get too technical, my brilliant scientist," Becky said as she stroked his neck softly. "We'll be there before the weekend is over. We can concentrate on other things then."

Becky purred as she gently rubbed her arm against Hugo's growing manhood in his pants.

Hugo gulped and Becky smiled. She stepped away and walked toward the SUV again. Hugo followed close behind.

They descended the other side of the mountainous area emerging on the northern outskirts of town. She drove for another thirty minutes until they reached a large farmhouse with a huge barn next to it. She had to drive slowly over a large ditch dug around the outside of the property. Hugo glanced at it briefly and discerned it curved slightly around the outside of the property. It seemed to intersect at some adjacent ditches that weren't quite as large and seemed to go through the center of the property. He wasn't able to discern the pattern as Becky pulled up next to the farmhouse and stopped.

"All the equipment you need is inside," Becky said.

"Oh," Hugo realized with shock. "I will need my files!"

Becky held up the backpack. "I've backed up all your data," Becky said with a wink. "It shouldn't take very long to transfer the data to the systems here."

"Good," Hugo said as he nodded and got out of the car.

They walked together into the house. Hugo found himself continually distracted by her sweet scent. He was like a schoolboy! All he could seem to think about was taking her to bed and ravishing her sweet body. He shook his head and took a deep breath.

Becky opened a door that led to the basement and went down. Hugo accompanied her and gasped as he saw the layout in the lower section of the house. The laboratory put his to shame with equipment he could only imagine owning. He stepped over to what he thought was his gene sequencer when he noticed it was a different manufacturer and even more powerful than the one he had in his own lab.

"My equipment is here somewhere?" Hugo asked. Becky chuckled.

"I told a little fib," Becky said as she plugged a device into a computer and typed a few commands into the system to start the transfer of files. "I just moved a few of your machines into a closet upstairs at your house."

"You tricked me?" Hugo asked and could feel the heat rising up his neck.

"Only to get you here where it's safe, darling," Becky purred as she walked up to him and gently stroked his chest. "Everything you need to succeed is right here and the police can't stop you if they can't find you."

Hugo began to relax a little. Her logic was flawless. Not only was she brilliant, but she had thought of everything. He realized he would indeed be more successful here than he would've been at his own home.

"Okay," he said as he caressed her cheek. "Let's get started."

Becky smiled and pulled him by the hand to a small refrigerator unit. She pulled out a small vial. The fluid within had a bright green glow. "I used one cc in the bat and two ccs in the guinea pig," Becky said as she handed him the vial.

Hugo looked at the substance and swirled it around for a moment. "We can use the centrifuge to infuse this into my delivery substrate. Boiling point?" Hugo asked as he walked to the centrifuge.

"One hundred and fifteen Celsius," Becky replied. Hugo nodded.

"Good. It will need to cure in the beaker without boiling for an hour," Hugo said. "You brought my supply from the house?"

"I brought all of it," Becky said as she looked down. "I knew they would confiscate it and I didn't want it in their hands. I knew you could make more of it if you wanted, but this way they would be starting at ground zero." Becky pointed at another refrigeration unit with an open cooler next to it. The appliance had a small magnetic heart stuck to the front of it.

Hugo smiled. "They won't get far. You can copy the data, but once you try to break the encryption, it will eat itself," he flashed a dark smile at Becky. "You're not the only one with secrets."

Becky held her hand to her mouth. Her heart skipped a beat and her face flushed. She had expected a somewhat more docile scientist at her beck and call. This would prove to be more exciting than she anticipated.

Hugo stepped over to the computer system Becky had

copied the files to and began working. He checked a few computations and nodded. He stepped over to the centrifuge and pulled out some of the test tubes. He gathered some of his vials and used a syringe to insert a specific quantity into each tube. He then repeated the process with a new syringe introducing Becky's growth and mass inversion serum. He set the centrifuge spinning.

Becky watched from a few steps behind him, but never interfered. As the centrifuge slowed to a stop, Hugo retrieved a third syringe and pulled one of the tubes out of the centrifuge. He pulled a small sample from the tube and walked over to one of the microscopes arrayed around the room. He selected a glass slide from a box and squirted a minuscule amount onto the slide. He put it under the microscope and observed the results. He stood up and looked at Becky.

"It works perfectly. You've used my samples before," Hugo said simply. "That's why some went missing weeks ago."

"I admit I did more preliminary work to get our samples to be compatible, but that's all," Becky said.

"Who are you working for?" Hugo barked as he stepped up to her and grabbed her shoulders. Becky gasped.

"I-I'm working for you," she whispered. "Since my first studies in Prague, I've followed you, followed your work. I just wanted to be with you and help you be successful."

"You were in Prague?" Hugo whispered and loosened his grip.

"I was a year or two behind you, but I heard Professor Bruzek sing your praises and I was intrigued. Once I met you on campus ten years ago, I knew I had to work hard to be worthy of being with you."

Hugo closed his eyes and took a deep breath. All he could see was her beauty and all he could feel was compassion mixed with an undeniable desire stirring in his loins. No woman had ever made him feel like this. He released her.

"I can't stay mad at you," he said with a sigh.

"You would be the first man who didn't," she said quietly.

Hugo frowned and gently put his hand on her face. He wiped away the tears that streaked down her face.

"I would never hurt you," he whispered as he lowered his face to hers and they kissed deeply. He fought the urge to push the equipment aside and take her right then on the table. He broke the embrace and caressed her face again.

"Let's get this serum cooking, shall we?" he asked. Becky smiled and nodded.

Hugo retrieved tubes from the centrifuge and walked over to a set of beakers set up on burners. He put each tube's contents into a separate beaker and turned on the burners at different heights. He grabbed an infrared thermometer and measured the heat for each one, slightly adjusting two of them. He set a timer on the computer for fifteen minutes and then stood by Becky holding her gently as they stood waiting for the timer to end. The embrace was warm and comforting, even though Hugo could feel his pulse increasing with every moment she was in his arms.

When the timer went off, Hugo released her reluctantly and turned off the burners. He used a long cylindrical glass piping to take a sample from each serum, cleaning it meticulously between each sample. He examined them all individually under the microscope.

"Sample A and B are sufficiently fused for use. The other two failed to combine," he stated.

"Do you want to test them now?" Becky asked.

"You have a test subject?" Hugo asked.

"Come," Becky said and held out her hand.

She led Hugo outside to the large barn behind the building. Inside, Hugo was amazed to find a single adult tom turkey. Behind the bird was a pile of feed for the it that must have weighed several tons barricaded behind a large solid fence and latched gate. The top was open and the height of the pile was easily visible.

"This is incredible," Hugo stated.

"Based on my own experiments, I know roughly the amount of feed needed to support the transformation. Of course, he'll stop eating voraciously once he's reached his full growth potential," Becky said as she swung her arms behind her playfully. "I realize there's a lot more feed there than we need for just this one experiment, but I figured we may have to repeat the process several times."

Becky walked forward and opened a small door at the bottom of the huge gate. A small quantity of feed trickled out onto the barn floor. "Plenty if he needs it," Becky said. She walked back to Hugo and draped herself on his arm. "You ready?"

"We have to document the process..." Hugo said as he deftly tried to work through the fog of desire that kept rolling over him.

Becky pointed at the ceiling of the barn. Four surveillance cameras pointed down at the barn floor centered on where the turkey stood. "Got it covered," Becky replied as she squeezed his arm.

"Yes," Hugo said as he cleared his throat. "Let's get started then."

"Wonderful!" Becky squeaked as they exited the barn.

Within a few minutes, they had returned with a syringe and Becky assisted by holding the bird as Hugo injected a small amount of the serum into the turkey's mid-keel pectoral muscle.

"That will aid in the slow dissemination of the serum through the body for a more distributed effect," Hugo said as he let go of the bird. Becky let go as well and the protesting fowl scurried away from them.

"How long will it take before we see results?" Becky asked.

"A few hours, I expect," Hugo replied.

"Plenty of time then," Becky replied as she grabbed Hugo's hand and pulled him from the barn. They secured the doors and made their way quickly to the house. Once inside, Hugo pulled Becky into an embrace she willing acquiesced to. They kissed passionately for several minutes before Becky pulled herself away and led Hugo upstairs to a bedroom that had wraparound windows displaying the barn a few hundred yard away.

Once in the bedroom, Hugo let the lustful thoughts and desires that had been building in his mind and body loose. They quickly discarded their clothing and fell onto the bed in a passionate embrace leading to furious lovemaking. After forty-five minutes of strenuous sexual activity, Hugo collapsed on the bed in a heap. Becky thoughtfully stroked his hair as he slumbered.

"So much kinder than the others," she sighed.

She watched the barn and jumped a little when the barn doors shuddered. She smiled and extricated herself delicately from Hugo's slumbering embrace. She moved quickly down the stairs all the way down to the basement. She turned on the monitors that connected to the cameras in the barn. A giant creature resembling a plucked turkey filled the room, madly consuming the large pile of feed behind the now broken fence and doors that had been holding it back. The feed was constantly refreshed from conveyor belts leading from several reservoirs below ground filled with tons of feed. Becky smiled as she thought about the congealed balls of feed that were set up to fall into the piles to be consumed by the ever growing beast before her eyes.

She pulled open a notebook and wrote out some calculations on the paper. She checked equipment measuring the weight of the turkey and checked her calculations.

"Time to wake our esteemed sacrifice," Becky murmured as she skipped happily back up the stairs.

She reentered the bedroom gently rolled Hugo onto his back. She carefully shackled his wrists and ankles as he groggily complied with her ministrations. Finally she worked the sheet off the bed from underneath him, revealing glowing, runic lines centered on the bed and leading to similar lines under the floor boards of the bedroom.

She worked Hugo's manhood to a stiffened state again and climbed on board. This final connection with his body finally roused the scientist from his nap.

"Becky, what's going on?" Hugo snapped as he tugged at the manacles tying him to the bed.

"Isn't it wonderful?" Becky replied. "You're the most important piece of tonight's ritual, my love."

As Becky continued to move herself on top of Hugo, the barn in the distance erupted as the giant form of a plucked fowl burst forth. Hugo's eyes got wide as he saw the beast wriggling atop the destroyed building, still moving its head toward the ground in search of more feed.

"It's finally happened!" Becky shouted. "A living creature large enough to accommodate the matter transference for our beloved god."

"What are you talking about?!" Hugo shouted.

Becky reached forward and grabbed a curved dagger from beneath the pillow and held it aloft. "You'll be spared gazing into his countenance and losing your mind, dear Hugo," Becky screamed in delight. "But the rest of the planet will be duly punished!"

Becky thrust the dagger into Hugo's chest, piercing his heart. As he jerked underneath her, Becky relished the feeling of his manhood shrinking within her as the last breaths escaped his body. Blood flowed from his pierced chest and dripped onto the runic lines, causing them to light up with an eerie purple glow.

The purple light traveled quickly through the lines on the floor of the bedroom. Outside, the trenches around the property flashed to life with the purple glow until they reached the turkey which had grown to the height of a twenty story building with a girth nearly as wide. The flesh of the turkey erupted with tentacles flowing forth into the surrounding air. Purple ichor flowed onto the ground as a hideous tentacled creature emerged from another dimension, changing places with the oversized fowl.

Becky's body writhed in ecstasy at the sight of the god emerging into her dimension. She erupted with insane laughter until an errant tentacle the size of a train engine whipped through the farmhouse utterly destroying it in a shower of splinters.

december

Night Town
Marshall Miller

"Why do I always get stuck with the late night shift?" Big Jim McCloud grumbled as he drove through the moonless night.

"Driving at night means we dodge the hot August summer sun in the Southwest. Especially in Texas."

Big Jim glanced sideways at the female figure in the front passenger seat. Once again, he was driving down back roads to save time and distance, all according to his sister Susan's plans. Fraternal twins, she still acted like she was years older and thus the "elder" in charge. Truth be told, he had been born first, a good minute before his sister.

But as much as they feuded and fussed, they still loved each other and always had each other's backs. That had been extremely important while he grew up gay. When no one else would come to his defense, being called "a queer" or "sick," Susan was always there. Later on, as he hit a tremendous growth spurt, he no longer needed her protection. And now, a semi-pro bodybuilder and powerlifter, no one dared call him a faggot. Now he was Big Jim.

So why were he and his sister not on better terms? Part

was due to their Red-Head Temper, both being gingers. But the primary reason was the young man seated behind them in the rental car.

Samuel Kant was a drag queen's drag queen, the epitome of the stereotypical mincing gay man as portrayed in Hollywood, television, and the butt of all those jokes in bars. And he was Big Jim's lover, his hopeful life partner. All his previous lovers and roommates had been other gay men are involved in weightlifting, bodybuilding, and martial arts. All had been a "man's man,"—macho to the extent that the women who hung around the gyms drooled over them.

Not Samuel. And this drove his sister nuts. After all these years of defending his homosexuality, Jim suddenly realized his sister had her own set of bigoted ideas and prejudices. As long as you fit her ideas of what was what, fine. If you did not, there was Hell to Pay.

"Fuck that," Jim had said on more than one occasion. "I love him; he loves me. Accept it!"

"He's a fucking wimp!" Susan had raged back. "He dresses in clothes I wear! My God, being attracted to other men is one thing. Being attracted to—to *that*! Who can't decide if he wants to be a guy or a gal! What are you, nuts?"

"No! I guess I'm just *sick*!" he raged back. "A *pervert*! As all those people said, when I was in school!" Then they would both storm off.

So now these three, and one other, were in route to a combination Body Builder/Mixed Martial Arts competition in Austin, Texas, having left Boulder, Colorado, hours before. Delaying their start time because Joseph could not get his butt in gear did not improve the situation.

Neither did Joseph's complaining about Texas in August.

And then, they had a stranger who made them feel they should hide all their conflicts.

Joseph Christopher, nicknamed by them "Holy Joe," was a divinity student who had answered an ad on the local college Internet Board for another rider to Austin. Susan was going to compete in a Mixed Martial Arts competition (her training probably started when she defended her twin years ago), and Jim in a Body Building competition, requiring registration fees, not to mention lodging expenses—so someone to share gas and travel expenses was a good idea. And Samuel was of little help, usually living off of Big Jim, pissing off his sister even more.

Jim had pulled Holy Joe aside and had braced him about the situation. "You're not going to lecture us about homosexuality being a sin. That we are all going to Hell, are you?"

Joseph had smiled. "Remember the idea of 'cast the first stone'? There is no way I am without sin. So me lecturing you about something between you and God that you do not hide would accomplish what?" Joseph was a dark-haired, slightly built college student who had a certain gravitas that belied his so-called pacifist beliefs. Jim saw in him a certain honesty and internal strength that he respected, despite their opposite beliefs in many primary areas.

Despite fundamental differences, he soon found that Joseph was a calming influence. Jim thought that someday they might even be friends.

Jim heard Samuel stirring in the seat behind him. He glanced in the rearview mirror and saw his boyish face, his coiffured blond hair. And again, felt the love he had for him.

Just then, Susan suddenly jerked awake in the front passenger seat. It took her a few moments realizing she was riding in the car and dreaming about something else.

"Where the Hell are we?" she asked.

"Saw a sign a couple of miles back said Nighttown, ten miles."

"Nighttown? I don't remember that on the map."

"Well, maybe, Sis, if we kept to the main roads instead of all these convoluted county and local roads…"

"The shortest distance between two points is a straight line. Wasting gas on a longer route just because they're 'main roads' is counterproductive to staying on budget."

Big Jim began to burn. "Do you always have to talk down to people? I know all about geometry. Neither my head nor my body is muscle-bound."

"Well then, you should understand saving money since two of us have to pay for a third."

"And we have a rider helping out. Quit your complaining about Sam. He's with me."

"Well then, quit complaining about my navigation. I'm the one doing all the planning—"

"Do you two always have to fight and wake everyone else up?" It was Samuel's voice from the back seat.

Susan's jaw tightened, and she spoke in a clipped tone. "Stay out of this. This is between my brother and me. If I want your opinion, I'll give it to you."

"Damn it, Susan—" began Jim.

"Oh, now the cunt gets bitchy!" Samuel always seemed to go for the jugular with his insults. And he always seemed to cause other people to suffer the results.

Susan's face turned bright red. In the blink of an eye, she had popped her seat belt and was going for Samuel in the back seat. "You fucking faggot!"

"Susan!" Jim yelled while trying to steer the car and grab

his sister simultaneously.

"Hey! What's—" Joseph started to say. Then the vehicle began to leave the road.

Jim tried to grab Susan, keep the car on the road, and yell all at the same time. He over-corrected with the steering wheel and sent the car to the opposite side of the road. During regular daylight hours, Jim would have hit oncoming traffic. In the middle of the night, he just put on a show of his inadequate driving skills.

The car went back and forth from opposite sides of the road, throwing up dust, dirt and gravel as Jim managed to hit both of the shoulders.

Suddenly, Jim slammed on the brakes, causing Susan to slam into him, pinning him to the steering wheel. Then the car stalled out.

All was quiet for a few moments as the dust cloud stirred up around the car settled. Then, unexpectedly, Holy Joe's voice was heard. "What are you? *Nuts?!*" Joseph yelled. He managed to open his door and jumped out. With surprising speed, Holy Joe was over at the driver's side door. He yanked the door open, and Susan fell out onto the ground.

"*You fools!*" Joseph screamed. "You almost killed us all! You—*assholes!*"

Bright flashing red and blue strobe lights suddenly illuminated the area.

"Ah, fuck," said Susan. "The cops."

Jim managed to extricate himself from behind the wheel. "I'll handle this."

The cop who exited the patrol car was almost as tall as Big Jim's six-foot-plus stature but was lither than the muscleman's bulky frame. Susan thought he moved like a dinosaurian raptor from one of the Hollywood epics, approaching them with single-mindedness behind mirrored sunglasses. Mirrored sunglasses at night? What the fuck was that?

"You folks havin' a heap of trouble, I see," the law enforcement official said in what was an accent that Jim could not quite place. He managed to make out the front plate of the police cruiser, which said Texas. Jim could have sworn he was still in the Okie Pan Handle.

"Sorry, Officer. I guess I dozed off at the wheel. No one's hurt. No harm, no foul." Jim tried to get his story out as fast as possible as he pulled his wallet out with his I.D.

That was when Jim noticed the officer's large nose holding up his sunglasses. And he was working it, sniffing it.

"I smell somethin' not quite right, Son." The cop sniffed loudly. "I think I smell some wacky Tobackey mixed with something else. Colorado plates too. You folks know *Mar-uh-juh-wana* still ain't legal in Texas, right?"

"Honest, Officer. No one's smoking anything. We're just—"

"I.D.," said the cop.

"—trying to reach Austin…" Jim let his statement fade as he saw the officer was not listening to a word he was saying as Jim handed him his driver's license.

Just then, Samuel made his continual mistake of opening his mouth and complaining with a bit of an exaggerated, affected lilt that he knew pissed off Susan. "That bitch hurt me!"

The cop, Jim's I.D. in his hand, quickly turned his head to look directly at the source of the annoying sound. The cop seemed to stare, his nose working again. Then he spoke. "What fruit tree did you just fall off of, boyo?"

Jim's face flushed. "Now look it, officer. There is no need to be rude!" As he said this, he heard Susan's snickering giggle.

The cop's head jerked back to look directly at Jim. "Statin' a fact ain't rude. Turn around. Put your hands on your head."

"Goddamn it, Officer!" Jim was suddenly fuming, his Red-Headed Temper getting the best of him. "What the fuck do you think you're doing? There's no reason for you—"

He never finished the statement as he was suddenly spun around and slammed into the side of the rental car. The lithe body of the cop held unexpected strength and speed. Handcuffs were clicked on his wrists in a blur of motion.

"Hey *fucker!*" Susan automatically jumped to her brother's defense and started to go all MMA on the officer's ass. She ran into a well-directed stream of pepper spray in her eyes. "Motherfucker!" Susan cried out as the extra intense concentration of cayenne pepper took effect and staggered back.

"That's the same kind as they use on bears in Alaska, Miss Big Mouth," the police officer spat out. "Should handle a butch dyke like you just fine."

The cop jerked his gaze to Joseph. "And you? You want somethin'?"

"No, sir! I'd like us all to take a Christian moment of peace, Officer—I didn't catch your name. Sir."

"Constable Black, Nighttown Township. Can you drive?"

"Yes, sir. My name's Joseph. Please to meet you."

"Load Fruitboy and Diesel Dyke in your car. Follow me to the courthouse. We all have a date with Judge Vlad at Night Court. If you take off'n me, I will smell you out, and track you down."

"Yes, sir." Joseph saw that Jim had left the keys in the ignition, then saw Constable Black frog march Big Jim to his patrol car and throw him bodily in the back. The officer slammed the door.

Samuel began blinking back tears. "Oh, isn't this just

fucking great! All the roads and towns and we had to pick the one with a gay-bashing pig as the Town Constable! Thanks, Susan!"

Susan, though nearly blind, with puffy eyes, still managed to slam a fist into Samuel's sternum, laying him out. She then stumbled to the back seat of the rental car and grabbed a bottle of water, and began dumping the entire contents into her eyes.

"You're a-comin'?" Constable Black's voice rang out.

"Yes, sir! Right away, sir!" Joseph grabbed Samuel and helped him to the front seat with unnoticed strength. Susan was lying in the back, discovering new uses and combinations of curse words. She would develop a whole new lexicon with the rate she was going.

As Joseph started the car and fell behind the Constables Patrol Car, he quickly began talking to his two tripmates. "Look it. Before I found God, I spent much time on the road. A lot of time in trouble. Small towns like this Nighttown are into revue enhancement. That means tickets, fines, and sometimes bribes.

"They *do not* want to spend time and money on incarcerating passers-through. So, please! Let me do the talking. Your bad tempers are about to get us into serious trouble, maybe a very bad beating and a dump in a ditch just for the fun of it. Understand?"

Between curses, Susan mumbled yes. Samuel managed to nod his head in agreement, still holding his stomach.

"Good. Hang on. This may be a bumpy ride!"

Joseph had trouble keeping the police cruiser in sight as it turned down a side road that had seen better days. Constable Black seemed to know where all the potholes were and expertly swerved around them at speed. Joseph had no such knowledge or luck, so he was soon far behind the police vehicle. Only that fact it was a straight shot to the alleged courthouse enabled Joseph and company to arrive only a short time after the Constable.

Joseph saw the Constable manhandling Jim out of the patrol car and caught a familiar sight. Jim had the bruise and indentation pattern of a "Screen Test," where the cop driving slammed on his brakes so that the unseatbelted handcuffed passenger would have his face and body slammed into the protective screen separating the passenger area from the front seat, which equipped older vehicles. Newer patrol cars replaced the screen with Plexiglas, leading to re-arranged dental work and noses.

Constable Black saw them pull up in front of the sizeable office-looking building that must serve as the courthouse and city hall. "Check in with the twin Bailiffs inside. Use the front door." He then continued to frog-march Big Jim in through a side door. Joseph led his two companions in thru the front double doors. As he did, he looked around what must be the Township proper. It looked like someone had built a movie set replica of a short Main Street USA circa the 1940s. There was even a faded old fashioned sign for a Soda Fountain and a couple of damaged World War Two Support Our Troops posters.

The three travelers went thru the doors and were met with a pale, tall, and slender woman holding a hand-held magnetometer in her hands.

"Empty your pockets and put them on the table. Any weapons?" The jet-black-haired woman spoke in an authoritative medium-toned voice. She had done this many times before.

Just then, an identical twin, dark uniform and all, walked in from another room. Joseph now saw why the Constable had said to check in with the twins.

A couple of minutes later, the three were sitting in a small courtroom, staring at a very high judges bench. Joseph had seen a lot of judges benches in his earlier travels, but none this tall. Someone wanted to impress any visitors with the gravity of the situation.

Constable Black came into the courtroom, pushing Jim in front of him. Around Jim's Neck was a reader board with his name, DOB, and a number written in grease pencil.

Susan started to stand up and say something. A firm hand from one of the twin bailiffs shoved her back into her seat on a bench. She began to curse when the Constables voice rang out.

"Don't be rude to the twins, Sheena and Shana. The judge don't like his daughters being Insulted."

Susan glared at him but shut up.

A rustling noise was heard from the area up and behind the extra-high judges bench. "Hear Ye, Hear Ye!" The twins' voices rang out in perfect unison. "All rise for the Honorable and Noble Judge Vlad Lupei. This Grand Court is now in session!"

As the twins finished, a tall, slender, jet-black-haired man in black court robes walked up behind the judges' bench. Joseph saw the family resemblance between the judge and the bailiffs.

The Judge nodded to Constable Black, then the twins. He scanned some papers that had been placed for his review.

"Constable Negrescu, or in English, Black. What can you tell me about these charges brought before me concerning this young man?"

"Well, Your Honor. Reckless Driving for crossing the center lane and nearly wrecking. Disturbing the Peace of the Township for the loud displays of temper. Contempt of this Constable by cursing and swearing—"

"Contempt of Cop?!" Susan yelled out, "What kind of kangaroo court is this?"

"Another outburst like that, it's twenty-five dollars or

twenty-five minutes in the Punishment Booth!" the judge snapped out.

Susan started to yell something else out, but Joseph jumped up. "Your Honor! May I approach the bench?"

The judge fixed him with his steely gaze. "Aw, we appear to have someone knowledgeable of and respects court procedures. Are you a member of the bar?"

"No, Your Honor. Just a flawed soul who has had his problems with the law. If I may please speak to you; I think I may be able to shorten these proceedings to everyone's benefit."

The judge smiled. "Yes. Please! I wouldn't say I like to waste my time on minor cases. So, approach the bench. You have a scent of honesty about you."

Joseph walked up in front of the high bench. He had to tilt his head to look up at the judge. "Your Honor. We are just tired travelers whose tempers have gotten the best of us. I ask that this Court recognize our failings and provide a way to pay for any slight or injury mercifully which we have caused to this Township and the constable. I am a Christian who feels a need, a calling if you will, to help my fellow humans. Thus I humbly ask you, Your Honor. Is there a payment, a fine, or a sacrifice I may make so that my companions may continue their journey?"

The judge grinned broadly, displaying a mouth full of large white teeth. "Aw, sacrifice! A word I do not hear often. A concept I have usually held close to my heart. So tell me, Mister—"

"Joseph Christopher, Your Honor."

"Aw, Joseph! A nice old name. So please tell me. When you mention sacrifice, do you mean it in an older, shall we say, Biblical sense?"

"Depending on the circumstances, yes, Your Honor. Jesus Christ sacrificed himself on the cross, showing no greater love for his fellow man and woman."

"So, Joseph. Would you be willing to sacrifice similarly for your fellow humans?"

Joseph did not miss a beat. "Yes, Your Honor. Given the right circumstances, yes."

"A proverbial pound of flesh, shall we say, Joseph Christopher?"

"To save them and their souls, yes."

The judges large nose was working a mile a minute, sniffing, snorting, as Joseph spoke. Then he laughed. "Constable Black! Observe an honest human! It is a pleasure to have made your acquaintance, sir. Now, how say you to a pound of flesh, a pint of your blood, and a crisp one hundred dollar bill as payment, sacrifice for the trouble your companions have caused?"

Before he could answer, Jim exploded and jumped up. "You sick bastard! What kind of judge talks about taking blood and flesh?"

Constable Black grabbed hold of the enraged Jim and tried to force him down into his seat.

"Young man, I smell the scent of dishonesty, selfishness, disrespect, and sick desire!" The judge's voice resonated throughout the Court Room.

"Your friend here is willing to sacrifice for what he believes in! For friends and family! Yet you disrespect that desire. What says you? What are you willing to give for your fellows?"

"Nothing to you, you sick fuck!" Jim's muscles were not just for show. Adrenaline-fueled rage coursed through Big Jim, and he snapped the chain on the handcuffs, throwing all his weight at the Constable. Strong though the Constable may be, mass acceleration has its strength. Jim slammed into Constable Black before anyone could react. The two figures collapsed back onto a wooden chair, shattering it. A loud, bellowing scream of pain echoed through the chambers as a sharp piece of wood impaled itself through the arm of Constable Black.

Susan leaped over the small fenced-shaped barrier that separated the gallery from the court bench area. She smacked into one of the Twin Bailiffs. Susan did a perfect Front Mule Kick into the Court Officers Chest, but it was like hitting an iron gate. She recovered and tried a Hook Kick to the Twin's Face. Her foot was grabbed by steel clamps that looked like hands. Susan screamed as the hands twisted the ankle and foot in angles they were not designed for, bones snapping audibly. The redhead collapsed to the floor.

"Order in the Court!" Judge Lupei yelled.

"Please! No! Stop!" Joseph yelled.

"You bitches!" Samuel screamed.

Jim broke free from the injured Constable, screamed in rage, and went towards the judges bench.

Suddenly, the judge snarled and leaped onto the flat raised wood in front of him. He then propelled himself past where Joseph was standing to match the action of any jungle cat. An opened mouth displayed way too many sharp canines as he landed on Jim and sank his teeth into the big man's throat. Blood spurted and began to spray as the judge ripped a large hunk of flesh from Jim's throat, then pushed himself off the man. Jim began to spin and run in a tight circle, much like a chicken with its head cut off. He collapsed on the floor, twitching as he bled out. Susan and Samuel both screamed.

Joseph was frozen where he stood. The judge, wiping blood from his mouth with his judges robe as he chewed and swallowed something Joseph did not want to think about, turned towards him.

"I guess you fellows have supplied the pound of flesh, young man," the judge said.

Joseph screamed and pulled his Cross from under his shirt. "In the name of Our Lord Jesus Christ, I command thee, Satan, get back!"

The judge barked a short laugh. "That only works on vampires who were Christian. We are neither. Bailiffs!"

"Yes, Father," the twins answered in unison.

"Escort all but *that* one," he pointed towards Samuel, "to the basement holding cell. Constable!"

"Here, Your Honor," Constable Black answered as he grimaced and pulled the small spear of wood from his arm.

"Take *that* one and the car back to where you found them. He has the smell of decay on him. I do not think he was cautious about his sexual partners."

Samuel began to scream. "Homophobe! Sick gay-bashing fuck! You will burn in Hell!"

Now it was the Constable's turn to laugh. "You think we ghouls care who porks who among you all Humans? Your dead pardner over there just had poor taste in mates. Should have had him checked out." The Constable sniffed loudly. "Ghoul's nose. The perfect health and truth screen." His broad smile had too many sharp teeth, prompting Samuel to shriek. The man then turned and ran. The constable laughed and ran after him.

"I'll fucking kill you!" Susan screamed at the judge while trying to stand on her ruined foot and ankle.

"Not in this lifetime," the twin bailiffs answered in unison.

"Sorry, young man," the judge said to Joseph. "I was willing to let you go for a pound of flesh and a pint of blood. But your Christ will be proud of your attempted sacrifice."

Joseph began to scream and shake as the bailiffs took him.

The sun was beginning to rise when Texas Ranger Andy Jackson saw the flashing red and blue lights ahead. He was headed to an early pre-trial conference in Amarillo; otherwise, he would not be driving down this county road.

As he slowed his car, he saw a Texas DPS Trooper standing near a stopped car and wrestling with someone. With smoothness bred from years of experience, Ranger Jackson was soon stopped, got out of the vehicle, and helped the Young Trooper.

"Trooper Smyth! See, you've got a live one!"

"Crazy asshole," the trooper answered as the two men finally got the screaming man handcuffed, then seat belted in the back of his cruiser.

"Here's his I.D., Ranger."

"Samuel Kant. Doesn't ring a bell. Run it, see if he has a record for being in a mental ward."

"Yeah. Found him locked in the trunk of that rental vehicle. There's no paperwork, no luggage, just this wacko and his I.D. Dispatch is trying to rouse the rental car agency.

Trooper Smyth chuckled. "He did scream something about Nighttown, about a Night Court, about a judge who ate people."

"Well, there was an attempt some twenty years ago to build a combination dude ranch, like a cheap permanent small movie set not far from here. The stated plan was to attract tourists and small film companies. The real reason was a Mexican cartel was trying to create a front for money laundering, not to mention a drug storage location and a hangout for them off the beaten track. An OCDETF investigation closed them down and seized the so-called town. I heard tell it was finally auctioned off to somebody from back East a couple of years ago. People around here say they see the supposed owners occasionally. Might be absentee owners, only checking in occasionally."

Ranger Jackson looked at the crazy man in the back seat, carrying on a loud conversation with himself.

"Colorado plates. Could be a drug deal gone bad."

"Yes, sir. Thought the same myself, Ranger."

"Well, Trooper, I'll see if I can find that old property on the way back from my pre-trial. You okay, taking this guy in by yourself?"

"Yes, sir. He's gonna wind up in the booby hatch by day's end anyway. Bet you a cup of coffee on it."

"That's no bet; that's a sure thing. I'll buy you a cup anyways. Be careful."

"Yes, Ranger. Always."

Samuel Kant screamed and carried on during the entire trip to the booby hatch.

It had been a sure thing.

thirteen

Thin Dog

Jennifer DiMarco

When winter crawls out of the woods and the sun rushes to set, when the days are short and the nights are long, this is when Thin Dog awakes. He stretches his long, thin body balanced on long, thin legs and from shadow to shadow he creeps.

The howling and the creaking isn't the song of the bare winter trees. It's Thin Dog. His body is so frayed that sometimes you can see right through it like a thread-bare blanket woven long ago from dark gossamer threads.

And if you look—if you *dare* to look—maybe you can tell from the way his head hangs low and the way he steps so carefully: He's looking for a friend.

There are lots of stories about slender creatures who stride on slender legs and steal with slender fingers. They wear fine suits with ties or they're covered in bark like ancient trees. But you know those stories aren't real. Creatures like that don't exist.

But dogs exist. Dogs are real. Even dogs as thin as mist and moonlight.

Thin Dog is old. Older than cities. Older than the tree roots where he tucks himself to sleep. He is worn thin by time and storms and rough, rocky roads which is why his name is Thin Dog.

In all his many ages and eons, he has seen everything: The dead ends of alleys. The under side of automobiles. Thrown rocks and sharp cans and cats so mean they'd scratch his eyes out... if he had eyes. He has seen war and famine, revolution and the rise and fall of regimes. He has seen seasons turn and extinction lay claim to more souls than he can remember.

Thin Dog doesn't want to see all these things. He doesn't want to wander the world or cross the seas or travel from street to street. But he does—never ending, always restless—because he's lonely. Because he's looking for someone. He's looking for anyone. And in a world with so many people and only one Thin Dog, you'd think his search would be short.

But people run away from Thin Dog. Children run away. Adults run away. Even other dogs run away. Thin Dog runs after them because he doesn't know why they're running. Is it his smooth face like a starless sky? Is it his paws of shredded midnight or his tail like a darning needle?

Thin Dog looks like a nightmare. And since everyone already has nightmares of their own, no one wants Thin Dog.

Once, he waited patiently. He watched as all the street lamps came on. He watched as the children left the park. He sat and hoped to be noticed. And he was. A small boy walked right up to Thin Dog.

Thin Dog was so excited that he leapt up and swallowed the boy whole without any trouble at all. Now the boy and Thin Dog would be together forever and neither of them would ever be alone.

Thin Dog slept all night with his belly full of his friend. He slept all through the next day, too. But when he woke the next night, the first thing he felt... was empty. One small boy simply wasn't enough.

So Thin Dog moved on. He raged with rivers and climbed over and under mountains. He met a girl tending sheep in a valley and he swallowed her whole. He swallowed the sheep, too, because they seemed lonely without their girl and he knew what loneliness felt like.

Once, he was swept away by a rogue tide and tossed on ocean waves for weeks or years. Another time, he washed up on a rocky shore and walked for months or centuries until he found a small town and swallowed a paperboy and all his newspapers.

In a large city, the young woman with the purple hair and big headphones never even saw Thin Dog before he opened his maw. And the businessman with his briefcase was gone in one swallow then another because he also held an umbrella and umbrellas are hard to swallow. Even the how-now brown cow took only one swallow.

Finally and at long last, on a particularly dark and stormy night, not far from where you are now, Thin Dog curled up in the thorny bushes alongside the road. He didn't sleep—he was too empty to sleep—but somehow he dreamed nonetheless.

He dreamed that he swallowed all the children in the world. The tall children and the short children. The children who laugh and the children who cry. The naughty and the nice children. He even dreamed of swallowing the children who were too grown up to believe stories about Thin Dog.

And in the dream, Thin Dog finally felt full.

He's right there, you know. In the shadows in the corner of the room. Look hard and you can see his smooth face. There behind the door or just below the window. Welcome him in. Give him a whistle. Call to him, "Come here, Thin Dog." Tell him, "You're a good boy."

Because he is.

author biographies

JANUARY

Daniel DiQuinzio is a freelance writer living in New Jersey. Born mentally and physically disabled, he holds a Master of Arts degree in history from Seton Hall University. He is a contributor to *Veteran Voices Newsletter*, *Marjorie Magazine*, and *Palm Coast Magazine*. His fiction has also appeared in *Real Love Magazine*, *Bohemian Renaissance*, *Urban Tymes*, *Sisyphus Quarterly*, *The Minority Report* and in *Naughty & Nice: Stories for Your Stocking*. DiQuinzio's poetry has appeared in *Sisyphus Quarterly*, *Sherlock Holmes Mystery Magazine*, and *Neurocentrikk* and his nonfiction has appeared in *Philadelphia Row Home*, *Palm Coast Magazine* and *New Jersey Monthly*.

FEBRUARY

D.L. Fowler is an award-winning historical fiction and historical nonfiction author with a focus on the life and times of Abraham Lincoln. He lives in the Pacific Northwest.

MARCH

Joe Nasta (ze/zir) is a queer multimodal artist and writer who works in Seattle and writes love poems. Ze is one half of the art and poetry collective Eat Yr Manhood and head curator of Stone Pacific Zine. Zir work has been published in The Rumpus, Occulum, Peach Mag, Yes Poetry, dream boy book club, and others. Joe's first book of poetry "I want you to feel ugly, too" came out in 2021.

APRIL

Dakoda Foxx is a writer, actor, artist, and paralegal. She is dedicated to making a positive impact on the people she comes in contact with. She advocates for people's rights and dedicates her life to help make a change for others. She hopes her readers see that there is light at the end of any tunnel, in any situation. Dakoda's memoir, *The Magic in the Nightmare that was Me*, is a story of survival, perserverance, and a spirit that refused to be broken. She has also written a pocket-sized book in the *Haunting of Orchard House* series called *Paranoia* and has contributed to the *Rise* poetry & short story collections *Resurrection (Volume 2)* and *Revolution (Volume 3)*. Dakoda's books are available at www.BlueForgePress.com. Find her on Facebook at: https://www.facebook.com/DakodaFoxxAuthorPage

MAY

Sami Ridge is a multi-disciplinary artist living in Seattle. Before migrating up the Pacific Coast, she became a published poet, having received first place in the Ina Coolbrith Circle Poets' Dinner Award (Nature Category), among others. In 2021 she released her first of two music singles to critical acclaim. Recently, she co-curated Stone Pacific zines 8th issue. She now splits her time between art modeling, painting, song & screenwriting, with the intent to release her first E.P., and take on her first film acting role, in the coming year. All of this can be watched from her Instagram, @samiridge

JUNE

Ellen Jordis Lewis lives in Portland, Oregon, with a rotating assortment of rescued creatures. Her short works have been published by Quick Fiction, Brilliant Corners: A Journal of Jazz and Literature, and The Jazz Fiction Anthology from Indiana University Press. She can be found acting up on twitter at @ellenjordis.

JULY

Author, illustrator, and award-winning actor and filmmaker, Maxwell DiMarco has been writing professionally since he was a pre-teen, with stories and novels published in *Tales of the Slug, Super,* and *Ghost Sniffers, Inc.* In addition to these family-friendly adventures, DiMarco has written stories for all four volumes of *Unnerving,* where he explores the darker aspects of society through both physical and psychological horror. He lives in the Pacific Northwest, where he works as a special effects editor and the host of the weekly children's series, *Seriously Cereal.* He is a huge believer in community, acceptance, and seeing the world from all perspectives, striving to always provide his readers with an intriguing, thought-provoking narrative, no matter the genre.

AUGUST

Bree Indigo is a poet and songwriter. She enjoys tarot, exploring Washington State's Olympic Peninsula, and tending to her menagerie of pets. She has been published in all five volumes of *Unnerving* and all three volumes of the women's poetry and essay collection, *Rise.* Indigo lives with her wife and their family in the Puget Sound. Her first memoir, *Unreliable Narrator,* is forthcoming from Blue Forge Press. Find her on Instagram @bree_indigo

SEPTEMBER

Pacific Northwest author Diane M. McPhee is a writer, painter, and mixed-media artist. Her three Detective Alan Sharp Mysteries, *Taken By Surprise*, *Capable of Murder*, and *A Possible Danger*, follow the detective on leads to solve dangerous cases while dealing with the fact that he may be aging out of the police force.

OCTOBER

Pauline Ugalde is a visually-impaired writer, gamer, amateur musician, and voice-actor. Her favorite genres are sci-fi, fantasy, and horror, and her creative influences are Stephen King, Mark Z. Danielewski, Toby Fox, and Daniel Mullins. Her favorite scary movie is *Get Out*.

NOVEMBER

Hailing from Tacoma, WA, Lauren Patzer has been an information technology guru, actor, writer and film producer among other pursuits. His love of horror began with a non-stop reading of *The Amityville Horror*. With two novels and over fifty short stories published now, his most recent work is the horror novel *Undead Reckoning*.

DECEMBER

Marshall Miller retired from Homeland Security and police enforcement to more deeply explore the human condition and what drives us a species. Framed with the arrival of alien Apex predators who see us as little more than a food source, Miller is best known for crafting his series, *The Tschaaa Infestation* that dares to ask: Are we truly superior and do we deserve to survive? Find out more about his work at www.tiny.cc/marshallmiller

THIRTEEN

A PNWC and Bumbershoot award-winning poet and Seattle Times bestselling novelist, Jennifer DiMarco first toured nationally as an author when she was nineteen years old, having written novels since the age of ten. The first sixteen years of her career included the publication of contemporary drama, high fantasy, science fiction, poetry, and mystery novels as well as the production of two short films and three stage plays. During a twenty-year hiatus from prose, DiMarco married, raised two children, and worked as a filmmaker writing and directing more than a dozen feature films, half a dozen mini series, and more than a hundred short films. She returned to prose with *Hannah at Night and Twelve Other Stories* in 2020. DiMarco lives in the Pacific Northwest with her wife, composer and actor Brianne, and their adult children, author and illustrator Maxwell, and actor and illustrator Faith.